Target:
The Bogeyman

AN EDWARD MENDEZ, P.I. THRILLER

BOOK 4

Gerard Denza

Target: The Bogeyman
An Edward Mendez, P. I. Thriller
Book IV

This novel is entirely a work of fiction. The names,
characters, and incidents portrayed in it are the work
of the author's imagination. Any resemblance to actual
persons, living or dead, events or locations, is entirely
coincidental.

Cover Art: Book Covers Art

Also available digitally.

BY THE SAME AUTHOR:

ICARUS: THE COLLECTED PLAYS

RAMSAY: DEALER OF DEATH

THE TIME DECEIVER:
An Edward Mendez, P. I. Thriller, Book I

NIGHT DRIFTER:
An Edward Mendez, P. I. Thriller, Book II

THE IMMORTAL:
An Edward Mendez, P. I. Thriller, Book III

TARGET: THE BOGEYMAN:
An Edward Mendez, P. I. Thriller, Book IV

Main Characters:

1) Edward Mendez: a private investigator who has two unusual cases to handle that may be more related than he imagines.

2) Yolanda Estravades: Edward's Olympic ice skating girlfriend who goes on a deadly date with her P. I. boyfriend.

3) Sergeant Tom Rayno: a dedicated police officer and a trusted friend of Edward.

4) Lieutenant William Donovan: a hard nosed but fair-minded police officer who is on a covert mission of his own.

5) Marlena Lake: a woman who has given refuge to a cold blooded murderer. She's in possession of information that terrifies even her.

6) Susan Broder: Marlena's daughter and a very sensible girl.

7) Victoria Mendez: Edward's beautiful sister who is afraid of the occult.

8) Nella Mendez: Edward's youngest sister who does his accounts for him.

9) Dottie Mendez: Edward's sister who is not afraid of the occult.

10) Catrina Mendez: Edward's acerbic sister who may be changing her attitude toward life.

11) Mrs. Isabelle Mendez: Edward's mother who possesses a knowledge of the occult.

12) Professor Frank Moreland: an astronomer and lecturer on the space-time continuum.

13) Mary Riley: Professor Moreland's assistant and former assistant to Professor Lange..

14) Henriette Miller: a nursing student at Hunter College who is now dating Lt. Donovan.

15) Josef Antonio: a man who has lived for two thousand years and who will stop at nothing to live forever.

16) Antonio's hitman: a young man with no mind of his own and no conscience.

17) Debbie Stone: a young teenage girl who is the Josef Antonio's next victim.

18) Grace Stone: Debbie's protective mother.

19) Teresa Farmer: a waitress and witness to a past crime that puts her life in danger.

20) Tommy Burton: a seven year old boy who is brutally murdered for no apparent reason.

21) Edith Burton: Tommy's grief stricken mother.

22) Jack Marino: elevator operator in Edward's building who is dissatisfied with life and falls in with the wrong people.

23) Maria Marino: Jack's eccentric mother.

24) Nathalie Montaigne: a Frenchwoman who has gone underground and is witness to a horrific crime.

25) Missy Wingate: an overweight woman who dies of old age at twenty-four.

26) Patty Kilmeade: a bakery owner who is killed for knowledge that she doesn't possess.

27) Erica Mills: a twenty-three year old woman who is dying of old age.

28) John Mills: a twenty-four year old man who has died of old age.

29) Jenny Sanderson: a friend of the Mill's couple who may possess dangerous knowledge.

30) George Sanderson: another friend of the Mills' whose life is now in danger.

31) Dr. Richard Aster: Erica Mills' attending physician at Mr. Sinai Hospital.

32) Dr. Claire Ingram: a no-nonsense doctor who gets on Edward's nerves.

33) Officer Patrick Mitchell: a veteran police officer with a solid right hook. He believes in justice and punishment.

34) Officer Roscoe Jackson: a young police officer partnered with Officer Patrick Mitchell.

35) Linda Kawano: a ruthless member of an occult group.

38) Kenneth Ng: leader of an occult group.

37) Rick Wasserman: member of an occult group who's real clumsy at killing people.

38) Jennifer Caswell: girlfriend of Rick Wasserman.

39) Freda Becker: member of an occult group and an ugly and bitter woman.

40) Hans Becker: brother of Freda Bauman and member of the same occult group.

41) Toni: a young girl who works in Patty's bakery.

42) Adam: the mailman in Edward's building and a natural snoop.

43) Alexandra Raymond: police stenographer and confidante of Lt. Donovan.

44) Eileen Kobe: a nervous and careless woman who has made a fatal mistake with a hatbox.

45 Louis Octavio: a methodical and untrustworthy man who never takes off his gloves.

Table of Contents

Part One Executions

Part Two The Hunt

Prologue One

MISSY WINGATE was waiting for the bus to arrive at the Grand Army Plaza transfer point in Brooklyn. She was one of several people standing at the bus shelter on a late Sunday afternoon. It was early September and the weather was a perfect day of sunshine and cool breezes. The summer of 1948 had been much cooler than usual. The nights had been downright chilly forcing people to wear a sweater or light jacket. The earth was still suffering the effects of the sun's disappearance back in December of last year; but, scientists were hopeful that nature would soon right itself.

The bus pulled in and Missy got on. People noticed Missy Wingate not so much because she was overweight, but because of the confidence with which she carried herself. Her doctor had told her just the other week that she bordered on obesity and had to lose weight; 99 pounds to be exact. This news came as quite a blow to the young woman who was all too self conscious of her girth and had already been dieting for as long as she could remember. She couldn't remember the time when she wasn't on a diet of some kind; for her, it was a way of life.

Missy found herself a seat on the bus and held on tightly to her shoulder bag and sneakers. She'd just been to the gymnasium and was now headed for home. She was tired but satisfied that she'd been able to keep up with the other members of her exercise class who all shared a similar weight problem.

Two young teenage boys were sitting opposite Missy as well as a young, black man. All three of them noticed the air of self confidence about Missy Wingate. And, they all stared at her as she left the bus. They didn't notice the slight stumble as she dismounted the steps at the rear of the bus. The accordion doors closed behind her.

Missy began the two block walk to the bakery. She was desperate for a cup of Patty's home brewed coffee. In spite of her euphoria, she was feeling tired...drained of energy; but, she would not let the outside world see this. However, the outward veneer was beginning to crack. Her stride wasn't as quick and worry started to show around her pale, blue eyes. Only a few more steps to the bakery. A cup of coffee is what she needed and maybe a slice of crumb cake...just for the sugar boost.

When Missy reached "Patty's Cakes," she had to step aside because a patron was coming out: a woman who was a little older than her: blonde and buxom. The two women nodded to each other. Missy entered the shop and the glass door closed behind her with the tinkle of small bells overhead. She almost collapsed into one of the wrought iron chairs.

Patty, the bakery owner, walked over to her friend. She looked at her friend's face and stifled a gasp.

-Missy? Missy, honey?

Missy didn't answer. She stared straight ahead as if in a daze. Now, she was in pain and her eyesight was blurring. Was someone standing near her?

-Yes?

-Missy? Are you all right? You look like you're ready to pass out,

Not waiting for an answer, Patty sat down opposite her friend.

-Can I get you something?

-Yes. Aspirin. Do you have any aspirin?

-I'll get you some from the back room. Just give me a second.

Patty got up and ran behind the counter to the back room where she kept most of the store's supplies. She knew she had aspirin there somewhere, but where? She wasn't the most organized person.

-Oh, my gosh! There in my purse.

She snatched her purse off of one of the supply boxes and dumped its contents out.

-Got 'em!

She scooped up the compact metal case of aspirin and ran back out front. Patty stopped to pour some coffee and, then, rushed to where her friend was. She screamed.

-Missy! Oh, my God! What in the world happened? Can you hear me?

Patty shouted out to her assistant behind the counter.

3

-Toni! Call an ambulance. Hurry!

Missy Wingate lay dying of old age on the bakery floor.

Prologue Two

ERICA AND John Mills were the perfect example of the perfect couple. They were young, upper-middle class people with nothing but opportunity and prosperity ahead of them. John Mills was a stock broker down on Wall St. and his wife, Erica, worked in the Publicity Department at a major publishing house in Manhattan. They enjoyed their work and had no intention of starting a family at the present time.

It was Sunday evening and they were expecting close friends for dinner: Jenny and George Sanderson, another perfect couple.

The Mills were in their new suburban home in Stuart Manor, Long Island. It was modern and, some would say, luxurious: two bedrooms, a living room, a den, a modern kitchen and even a study with a built-in book-shelf and a television set. John Mills was in that study now, leafing through a book on economics. His wife, Erica, was in the kitchen fixing canopies for their guests. Neither husband nor wife were feeling well. John Mills was no longer looking at the printed words in his book. He was looking at his hands that were now inexplicably aged with liver spots. He dropped his book to the floor, not just upon seeing his hands, but because he could no longer read the words on the printed page. John Mills tried picking up the book. He did; but, he could not straighten up. He tried once again to stand up straight, but wrenched his back in the process. He cried out in agony as he collapsed on to the carpeted floor.

Erica Mills' hands started to tremble. The canapé in her hand fell into the silver tray. Her breathing was becoming strained and she started coughing...a dry, hacking cough that almost strangled her. In a few moments, the cough subsided, but her body felt so weak that her movements seemed almost feeble.

-Oh! What in the world is happening to me?

Her voice sounded different: old and witch-like. She tried calling for her husband.

-John! John!

Her hand went to that sore spot at the back of her neck that had been bothering her since yesterday. It felt like an infection. Had she been bitten by some horrible insect? Erica had a fear of insects. Yesterday, at the fun house in Coney Island, she-

Her thought was never to be completed as she collapsed to the kitchen floor as that same hacking cough came back.

Jenny and George Sanderson arrived on time for dinner; but, no one was answering the front door.

-Isn't their house beautiful? I just love what Erica's done with the shrubbery and the front lawn.

-It sure is nice enough; but, I'd like to see the inside of the house, too. Jenny, why don't I go around back to the kitchen? Stay here, just in case.

-Okay, but hurry. They might have been called away on an emergency. It's not like Erica to keep guests waiting.

George went around to the back of the house and tried peering in through one of the kitchen windows. The lights were on and he could just make out the tray of canapés on the counter.

-Where the hell are they?

He spotted the body on the floor, but didn't recognize who it was. He ran to the side of house.

-Hey, Jenny! Come here, quick, and have a look.

Jenny ran as fast as she could in her high hells, fighting back a cold spasm of fear.

-What is it? Anything wrong?

-There's a woman on the floor, I think. I don't like the look of it. Who is she? Can you make it out?

George didn't recognize the sound of his own voice. It sounded strained and unnatural.

Jenny stared real hard at the figure lying motionless on the floor. It couldn't be...it just- The apron that the woman was wearing was the one Jenny had given Erica.

-Oh, God! George, see if the door's open.

He tried the handle. Locked.

-Break the glass. For god's sake, break the glass!

-What the hell's got into you?

-Don't you recognize her? That's Erica on the floor.

George had a hard time taking that in. He broke the glass pane on the door and jerked open the handle. Jenny practically shoved him in. They knelt by the prone figure. She was still alive.

-Erica? Erica, is it you? What in the world happened?

Erica tried speaking.

-I didn't hear you, honey. George, what did she say?

-I couldn't make it out. Erica? Erica?

-Don't shout at her.

-I'm gonna' call an ambulance. Where the hell is John?

-Never mind about him. Just dial the emergency number. The phone's on the wall over there.

Jenny turned her attention back to Erica.

-Erica? George is calling for help.

-Jenny?

-Try not to talk.

-Yesterday at...the shadow came...a phantom...felt like an insect...

-I don't understand. What shadow? What are you talking about?

Erica Mills lapsed into unconsciousness.

Prologue Three

JACK MARINO stepped out of the subway kiosk and began to walk toward his workplace. He was a young man of nineteen and in pretty good health. He'd done some amateur boxing at the local gym and even worked with the free weights when he could.

Jack hadn't finished highschool. He dropped out when he was sixteen and wasn't too particular about what job he happened to come upon in the want ads. He had done messenger work, maintenance work and many odd jobs to help out his mother at home: a mother who told fortunes and read tea leaves for the neighbors. And, when she wasn't indulging in fortune telling, she worked in a sweat shop near the garment district. It didn't pay much and she wasn't a particularly dedicated worker.

A few months ago, Jack decided to leave home and find his own apartment. He did. A studio apartment in the back of a tenement building in Brooklyn. And, he could barely afford the rent. In short, he realized how limited his choices were in life. As much as he hated to admit it, he just might have to move back in with his mother. Life was tougher than he thought.

Jack wasn't in a hurry to get to work today because he'd have some explaining to do. People were bound to notice the bruises on his face and ask questions. What could he tell them? Not the truth. Not if he valued his life. Best to face it when he had to.

He looked over his shoulder. That gray van was still dogging him. Why? Was it part of their way of keeping an eye on him? He didn't think so; but, he picked up his pace anyway. Only a few more blocks to Fulton St. and his job. He'd be safe there, wouldn't he? Maybe, he should talk to Mr. Mendez? No. It was too late for that.

Too late? What was it too late for? He didn't know. He couldn't remember. His memory was...failing him? What had been said to him just yesterday before he was set free? It was just coming back in fragments...like a dream you can't remember but one that haunts you all day because it's just on the rim of consciousness.

The bright, overheard light. The figures of people whom he couldn't quite make out. He could see what they were wearing, but couldn't see their faces. Were they circling about him? He didn't know. He couldn't tell. His sense of direction and reference points were all distorted. The one man kept speaking to him...asking him questions...never letting up. What kind of an accent did he have? There was an accent, but it was masked by the man's perfect English...his grammar...the stress points on his words...it all ran crystal clear as it penetrated Jack's conscious mind.

-You are known as Mr. Jack Marino.

Was that a question or a statement? Jack wondered that as he sat bolt upright in his chair. He wasn't tied up, but his will to move had somehow been taken away from him.

-I'm Jack Marino.

-It took you long enough to answer. You work in the same building as Mr. Edward Mendez, P. I. Verify what I've just stated.

-Yes. He's my friend.

-Is he? How have you benefitted from Mr. Mendez' friendship?

-I don't know what you mean. We're friends.

-You are of the lower-middle classes. Your future is that of a laborer. I believe blue collar worker is the expression. You are nineteen and your life will not be at all interesting.

-It might be.

-It won't; not as things now stand with you.

-How are you gonna' change it?

-Was there a note of defiance in your voice.

-What of it?

-We will provide you with money, Mr. Marino.

-What's it gonna' cost me?

-You're familiar with the term: "no such thing as a free lunch." Good. You are no fool. The price of admission to wealth is relatively easy. I must pay Mr. Mendez's office a visit and help myself to his files. You will "cover" for me. No one will be harmed; least of all Mr. Mendez.

-Why can't you just ask him for his files?

-That would never do. He's too inquisitive…much too inquisitive.

-And, that's all I have to do?

-For now. More will be asked of you later.

-You got a name?

-My name is Mr. Kenneth Ng.

-Well, Mr. Ng, just suppose I say no? Why should I do any of this?

-You've just had an assignation with a civilian member of the United Staes military; is that not correct?

-I don't know what you're talking about.

-The assignation was one of a homosexual nature. Don't bother denying it. We know of your tastes in men.

-What are you telling me?

-You will do as we want you to do, Mr. Marino. Your meeting with this man was a very dangerous thing for you to do. He is involved in certain covert operations for your government. He has much to lose and so do you. Am I making myself clear, Mr. Marino. Knowing this man puts your life in danger.

-How do you mean?

-You were paid for your services. Don't deny it. We will also pay you and we will keep you alive.

Silence for a few moments.

-Mr. Marino, we will release you soon and your memory will be selective. Do you understand? No. You don't. More than likely, a gray van will follow you and you may even notice this from time to time. Ignore it. The sooner we accomplish our goal - with your help, of course —the sooner that gray van will pose no danger to you.

Another silence.

-And, by the way, you will not remember this conversation...only fragments of it.

Part One
Executions

Chapter One
Thursday Morning,
September 2, 1948 Grand Central Station

IT WAS Thursday in New York City and the day was almost warm, but the air still had that persistent chill in it. He walked into the former office building of Professor Charles Lange. Why he was doing this, the P. I. wasn't entirely sure? Who would he find in Professor Lange's office if anyone? His secretary, Mary Riley, might still be there and Edward was counting on that.

He pressed the "up" button on the elevator and waited. The P. I. noticed the book store just off to his right. He wondered what kind of books they sold. Probably, the strictly academic kind. Maybe, he'd have a look on his way out.

The doors to the elevator opened up. He got in and headed up to the third floor. When the doors opened, he stepped out and was greeted, in a manner of speaking, by none other than Mary Riley herself. She had only glimpsed Edward Mendez on Liberty Island as he was being led into the ferry boat. They hadn't spoken. At the time, she was overcome with grief at the death of Professor Charles Lange. It was only later that she learned of how he was killed and why. She was still coming to terms with her former employee being not only a traitor to humanity but a Nazi sympathizer.

-Miss Riley?

-Yes?

-Edward Mendez.

-I do recognize you, Mr. Mendez. Please, come in.

Edward followed the efficient secretary into the outer office. She sat behind her desk and beckoned him to sit down.

-Now, Mr. Mendez, how can I help you?

-Have all of Professor Lange's records and documents been removed?

-Yes. The authorities came the very day he- died. They were quite thorough. There's nothing left. You can go into his office and check for yourself.

-I believe you, Miss Riley. The U. S. agencies are quite thorough to the point of being brutal.

-That's an excellent way of putting it.

Edward hesitated.

-Mr. Mendez? Why not just say what you came for?

-Has Professor Lange been replaced by anyone.

-Yes. The foundation appointed a Professor Frank Moreland. Why do you ask? Are you interested in science?

-Sort of. I have a few questions I'd like this Professor Moreland to answer; that is, if he can.

Mary Riley was a shrewd and perceptive woman: something was bothering this handsome man…something was preying on his mind. And, she wanted to know what it was.

-Professor Moreland isn't in right now. Mr. Mendez, I'll be frank. I'm still upset about the events of last December. I don't blame you for what transpired; but, surely you can be forthright with me now. What is on your mind?

Edward thought about it for a second before deciding.

-Last April back in '47, Miss Riley, something pretty strange happened to me. I suffered a memory lapse of a few hours and for the life of me, I can't come to terms with it. If you must know, it's been dogging me for months now.

To his utter surprise, Edward told her of his complete loss of memory when he had awakened on the slab of ice in midtown and how he eventually got back his own identity with the exception of those few hours between dusk and night.

-But, Mr. Mendez, shouldn't you, perhaps, seek the help of a medical doctor? Why a scientist?

-I found something in my office that, I think, implicated Professor Lange.

Mary Riley sat forward in her chair.

-In heavens name, what?

He told her about the photographs of the atom bomb testing and the white "specks" in those photos. He couldn't help but trust this woman. And, besides, he knew that the authorities had had her thoroughly checked out.

-How fascinating. And, you don't remember having obtained those photos or even writing those names on the back of one of them?

-Not a clue. So...Miss Riley, would you happen to know when Professor Moreland is due in?

-Yes. I'm afraid it's not until next Monday. He's taken a few days off on account of the Labor Day weekend. I never take time off myself. And, I've been criticized for it.

-Tell your critics to mind their own damned business. You could come to work for me anytime. Could you schedule me an appointment for next week?

-Of course. Would Thursday at 9 A.M. be good for you?

-It'll be perfect. And, by the way, what is Professor Moreland like. If you don't mind my asking.

-Very distinguished and neat as the proverbial pin. He's in the middle of writing a book on the continuum of time and space. I've proofread a couple of chapters. It's very good.

-When it comes out, I'll get the professor to autograph a copy for me.

Edward got up to leave.

-Miss Riley, I'll see you and Professor Moreland next Thursday. And, much thanks.

-Goodby, Mr. Mendez.

On his way out of the building, Edward forgot to look in on the bookstore. He was deep thought and didn't notice the man in the dark gray suit staring at him.

Edward Mendez was walking down Vanderbilt Avenue toward Grand Central Station. It was mid-morning and he was smoking the last cigarette in his pack of Lucky Strikes. He'd have to stop off and pick up another pack. His hand reached into his suit jacket. It touched his shoulder holster holding his Waltham P 38 semi-automatic. He had on his new dove-gray suit that his girlfriend, Yolanda, had picked out for him.

Yolanda Estravades was waiting for Edward in her apartment on 23rd St. that he now frequently shared with her. At the figure skating national championships that year, she had won a bronze medal which got her a spot on the Olympic team. She was thrilled and did well at the Olympics, but did not medal. She placed sixth overall after having faltered on the required "figures." Yolanda was now determined to stick it out for at least one more season as an amateur to claim the National and World titles. At the World's, she had placed fourth. She had cried for days afterwards.

Edward was about a half a block from the side entrance to Grand Central. He didn't notice the four people who were hurrying inside to catch the crosstown shuttle train. Had the P. I. noticed them, it wouldn't have made any impression. He hadn't met any of them except for the middle-aged woman who was with them.

Grace Stone and her teenage daughter, Debbie, had finished shopping for some school supplies. Mrs. Stone had also taken along her seven year old nephew, Tommy Burton. And, a recent family friend had also made the trip from Brooklyn: Nathalie Montaigne, a Frenchwoman who Grace was impressed with. She liked her knowledge of the world and was impressed by her good common sense. The woman was friendly without being too familiar.

They entered the terminal and began the climb down the marble stairwell to the main floor. A man had been waiting for them by the same side entrance. He drew a gun from the pocket of his trench coat and took aim at his target. He fired the gun. The bullet ripped through little Tommy's head, killing the boy even before his lifeless body hit the steps.

Without giving anyone time to react, the assassin took aim at his next target: the teenager, Debbie Stone. But, the young girl rushed forward to help her stricken cousin upsetting the assassin's aim. He had to shift his line of vision. And, now, the crowd of commuters started reacting: people were screaming and rushing forward to help. Nathalie Montaigne had enough presence of mind to turn in the direction of the fired shot. The Frenchwoman saw the man taking aim at Debbie and screamed.

-Someone, stop him! He's going to shoot!

Edward Mendez heard the gunfire and rushed head-long into the terminal with his gun drawn. He saw the assassin taking aim at Debbie Stone. Edward fired and hit the assassin in the shoulder. The assassin staggered forward but held on to his balance and his gun.

Edward ran to overtake the man who had jumped down the flight of stairs and was now pushing his way through the crowd of commuters. The P. I. was hot on his trail, but the assassin was weaving his way through the crowd with an uncanny skill: merely grazing people as he passed them…slithering along like some snake. Edward had to shove his way through until he cleared the crowd. He was only a few feet from his quarry.

Two men running through Grand Central. They were passing the central information kiosk and heading toward the ramp that exited on to 42nd St. The assassin was about halfway up the ramp and Edward was just about to start the climb. The assassin turned about and took aim at the P. I. and fired. Edward ducked down and the bullet just missed him. He struggled to his feet as his assailant ran out the exit door.

The P. I. got up and followed, but was too late. The assassin had vanished into the crowd and was lost from sight. Edward retraced his steps back to the scene of the murder. The police and the medics had arrived. He spotted his old friend, Sgt. Tom Rayno, and walked over to him.

-Hello, Sergeant Rayno.

-Edward Mendez, pal. Don't tell me that you're in on this case already.

-Not officially. I'm just one of those innocent by-standers that gets shot at.

-Where did you lose him?

-By the ramp leading out on to 42nd St.

Sgt. Rayno looked in that direction.

-It's a long shot; but, I'd better have a look. Keep my two boys company, will you?

Edward waved to the two police officers who waved back.

-I will. And...the little boy who was shot. Is he...

Sgt. Rayno shook his head.

-Dead. Didn't know what hit him, poor sap. His aunt and cousin are taking it pretty bad. But, the older woman seems okay.

-Good. I'll go over and have a talk with her. Mind?

-Me? Nope. But, you-know-who might.

Edward grinned.

-Lt. Donovan. We'll just keep this between ourselves for now. And, you better get going. I don't think the bastard's waiting around for you.

Sgt. Rayno walked off and Edward ducked under the police tape set up to preserve the crime scene and keep out the crowd. The medics were placing the dead boy on the stretcher and covering his body

Grace and Debbie Stone were being let up the stairs to a squad car parked outside on Vanderbilt Avenue. Edward approached the middle-aged woman who was getting ready to leave the crime scene. She looked more ill at ease than anything else. Her back was to Edward whom she had immediately recognized. It was too late for her to run; but, did she dare face this man? Perhaps, he would not recognize her? His girlfriend, Yolanda, would; but with a man one never knew. Nathalie braced herself and turned to face the shamus.

Edward didn't at once recognize Nathalie Montaigne. Her appearance had been altered from that of a woman in her late forties, who was fighting every year of advancing age, to an older woman of sixty-five. She saw that the Edward had recognition in his dark, brown eyes.

-Madame? Are you a witness to this crime?

She had to answer and her French accent would surely give her away.

Edward continued to address her.

-If you are, we can both wait for Sgt. Rayno to return. I don't think he'll be long.

He waited for her to answer and- of course! The eyes...not as heavily made-up as they had been back in December when they came across as dark and malevolent.

Edward grinned at her.

-What's the matter, lady? Afraid I'll recognize your French accent, Miss Montaigne?

This private detective was sharp. Nathalie could almost like him.

-As you say in America: "the jig is up." I have been caught; trapped, if you would.

Edward had to ask his next question.

-What the hell are you doing here? I'd have bet ten-to-one you'd be hiding somewhere in Europe by now with your partners in crime.

-I like your country. And, I have committed no crime.

Edward hooted at that one.

-No crime, huh? Attempted murder and theft? I could have you sent up for ten years. I think I will.

-No. You cannot. I beg of you.

Nathalie took a handkerchief from her purse.

-What I did, I was forced to do. They would have killed me if I had not made the attempt. Professor Lange would have exposed me. I heard about his death and good riddance to him. You did a good job of killing him.

Edward turned around to see if Sgt. Rayno was coming back, but too many commuters were blocking his field of vision. He turned back to Nathalie who continued her diatribe.

-We played the game as equals, Mr. Mendez, and I lost. Please, do not send me to prison. Look at me. I am old and that's not an easy thing to admit.

-Where's Werner Hoffman? He's been helping you out, right?

-Yes. And, he is back in his beloved Germany. And, I will tell you this: he sends me a monthly stipend; that is how destitute I am.

Edward thought it over for a second. Nathalie wanted to say something more; but, she didn't want to overplay her hand. The words she next spoke were chosen with great care.

-Mr. Mendez, I betrayed you once. It will never happen, again. I swear it on all the saints. And, we can help each other. Your sister-

Edward interrupted.

-How?

-I saw who murdered the young boy. I know of the circumstances behind it.

-You better catch your breath. You're starting to hyperventilate,

-A cigarette, please. Do you have one?

He flipped her a a cigarette, lit it for her and helped himself to one.

-Nathalie, I can't let you walk away from here.

She took a deep drag on her cigarette.

-I've no intention of doing that. I will tell all that I know at police headquarters. I only ask that you do not expose me.

Edward blew smoke in her face.

-You're a fine one to ask that. Okay. I'll hold back for now; but, I'm not promising you a damned thing. Here comes Sgt. Rayno.

Jack Marino was standing in the elevator that he'd driven up and down at least fifty times that day. He didn't mind because he liked his job and, for the moment, life was easy and simple enough...or it had been. Deep inside, the nineteen year old felt the stirrings of wander lust. He liked working in downtown Manhattan right in the middle of the financial world and Wall St.: physically so close, but as far off as the center of the Milky Way galaxy.

Tonight, he was looking forward to a homemade dinner at his mom's place in the East Village. She was a good cook and kept a clean house. And, she wanted her son to come back home. Mrs. Marino was a woman who didn't like living by herself, and she was also desperate for money.

Jack was awakened from his reverie.

-Excuse me? Tenth floor, please.

-Oh! Sorry about that. Just getting ready for the mad dash office crowd.

-Of course. May we go on up, now, or will you keep me waiting?

-Sure thing.

The tall man got in and Jack closed the accordion elevator doors. His passenger was Asian, tall and well dressed. And, Jack could tell when someone didn't want to make conversation so he left his passenger to himself.

-Here's your floor, sir.

-Thank you.

Before Jack could close the elevator doors, the man turned to speak to him. He took off his hat and lowered his scarf. Jack took a step back.

-Mr. Ng. I didn't recognize you. I'm real sorry.

-Don't be. I didn't intend for you to recognize me. I will see you later, tonight. And, someone is buzzing for you. Better answer it. And, remember, come back for me within five minutes time.

Jack didn't scare too easy, but this man's voice was hard and clipped and menacing. And, he saw the man — Mr. Ng — knocking on Mr. Mendez's office door.

There was no answer. Good. He hadn't expected there to be anyone in the private investigator's office. Mr. Ng took out the skeleton key and placed it in the door's lock. It opened and he walked into Edward Mendez's office. Of course, he didn't turn on the overhead light. He saw the file cabinet behind the desk and made for it. He was methodical as he went through the filing drawers one by one starting from the top.

Mr. Ng opened the bottom drawer and went through the files. He found what he had been looking for: the photos of the nuclear detonation and the specks of white light that were not white light. No. He knew what they were because he had witnessed these space craft landing. Mr Antonio had ordered him to get the photos because they could be useful as protection for the group.

-I wonder if Mr. Mendez knows of the import of these photos? I doubt it. If he did, he'd have them under lock and key or placed in a bank vault. But, that is not my concern.

Mr. Ng closed the file drawer and placed the file folder in his attache case. Before leaving Edward Mendez's office, he tried looking through the frosted glass window to see if anyone was about in the hallway. It wouldn't do to be seen walking out of the P. I.'s office.

No one was about. Mr. Ng left the office and rang for the elevator.

Mr. Josef Antonio had gotten his breath back and was no longer dodging pedestrian traffic. He was still walking at a brisk but socially acceptable pace that wouldn't call attention to himself. Yes. It was a pleasant day, although a little too chilly for this time of year; the early onset of Autumn, perhaps. He didn't really care.

Mr. Antonio reached the corner of 55th St. and Ave. of the Americas where he hailed a cab and gave the driver directions for the upper east side. Yes. He was heading for 1st Ave: a town house discreetly tucked away so as to be as inconspicuous as possible. The perfect hide-out for the near perfect criminal.

Mr. Antonio sat back in the comfort of the cab. Traffic was heavy along Avenue of the Americas but this didn't matter. He had plenty of time and needed to regain his senses, so to speak. He'd made good his escape and that, of course, was satisfying. A pity that Edward Mendez of all people had shown up when he did. Rotten luck, that. No matter. He knew where Debbie Stone lived and Miss Nathalie Montaigne. The both of them would have to be killed, of course; but he mustn't give way to panic. No emotion and no conscience were indispensable to his trade. Some would ask why he simply didn't go to their residence and do the job under cover of night. How pedestrian that would be. No. A demonstration of power in broad daylight to rattle the nerves of the police and any bystander that had the misfortune of witnessing his crime.

The taxi was now headed crosstown. He'd have to make contact with his group later that evening when he could issue instructions to them. He was almost tempted to doze off in this cab. And, thank God this cab driver was not the talkative kind. How he loathed incessant chatter from these cab drivers.

Within the half hour, the taxi pulled up in front of Marlena Lake's town house. He would have plenty of time to rest before cocktails and dinner. He paid the cab driver and gave a not-too-generous tip: a habit that he'd picked up from Marlena's daughter, Susan: a very sensible girl. A pity that she was on the plain side.

-Thank you, Miss.

-You're welcome. Have a pleasant day.

Josef Antonio entered the townhouse as Isolde Himmel. He had his own set of keys that he now took from his purse. He had discarded his trench coat and pants in the rest room of a small mid-town restaurant that he often patronized. He completed his disguise with carefully applied make-up and the articles of feminine clothing that had come out of the trench coat's lining.

After months of planning, the job was only half complete...no...a third complete thanks to that damned shamus. Perhaps, Mr. Mendez should be attended to? No. Antonio didn't kill for mere sport. He killed for a reason and that reason was survival.

He entered Marlena's living room. No one was about. A plan was hatching in his ancient and murderous brain as he sat down in one of the two armchairs. Antonio's accomplice had to be contacted and this could not wait until the evening hour.

Chapter Two
Thursday Late Afternoon, September 2, 1948
More Questions Than Answers

EDWARD, SGT. Rayno, Mrs. Grace Stone, Debbie Stone, and Nathalie Montaigne were assembled in Interrogation Room I on the third floor of the 86th precinct. Edward and Sgt. Rayno sat at opposite ends of the table facing each other. Mrs. Stone and her daughter, Debbie, sat next to each other to Edward's right and Nathalie Montaigne sat to the P. I.'s left.

All five people had a coffee container in front of them. Nathalie Montaigne hadn't touched hers. She preferred water, preferably with ice in it. This time, she didn't get any ice.

Sgt. Rayno kicked things off.

-I've just had a call from Lt. Donovan. He's on another case uptown and can't be here; but, he'll be spearheading this case.

He turned to face Mrs. Stone and her daughter, Debbie.

-I've already had statements from you, Mrs. Stone, and Debbie. If you like, you can leave; but, I'd prefer that you'd stay.

-Why, Sergeant? My daughter is very upset. It's been a terrible day and I still have to tell young Tommy's mother-

-That's being done, Mrs. Stone.

-I should do it and not some stranger. It will be a terrible blow to her.

-I know. And, I'm sorry that it has to be that way. But, Miss Montaigne over here has yet to give her statement and I'd like you to hear what she has to say. It may jog your own memory.

The door opened up and an attractive young woman walked in carrying a stenotype machine.

-Oh. Here's the stenographer. Miss Raymond? You can set up over there right next to Miss Montaigne.

-Sorry I'm late, Sergeant.

-No problem. Let me know when you're ready.

And, in a moment, the efficient Miss Raymond had her stenotype machine set up and was ready to make a verbatim transcript.

-Sgt. Rayno? I'm ready when you are.

-Thanks, Miss Raymond. Okay, Miss Montaigne? Let's have it from the beginning.

Nathalie had prepared herself for this. It had been several hours since Tommy was murdered and the waiting time had been put to good use. She would be completely honest. Why not? If the murderer had seen her glimpse him, her own life was in danger. If he could kill a little boy, he'd certainly have no compunction in killing her.

-Of course. It began several months ago when the sun vanished for a time. It was a December night and I was looking for transport into the city. I found myself at the Crescent St. train station near Highland Park. That's where I first met Grace and Debbie.

Nathalie took a sip of water and continued.

-A man had thrown himself on to the tracks. We thought he'd been killed. The medics had even covered his face. It was a ghastly sight...blood had soaked through the sheet. Horrible.

Sgt. Rayno interrupted.

-He wasn't killed. He died later under pretty unusual circumstances. Are you aware of that, Miss Montaigne?

-No. I'd no idea.

Edward asked the next question.

-How many of you were waiting inside that train station?

Nathalie shook her head.

-I don't know. I didn't think to count.

-Take a guess.

-I would say about a dozen people. Grace, do you recall?

-About a dozen. It was a small waiting room and it was crowded.

Debbie spoke up in a strained voice.

-Tommy said he counted thirteen people including all of us. He was always looking around and studying people and wondering about them.

Edward pursued his line of questioning.

-Did anyone stand out from the crowd? Did anyone act out of the ordinary? Think, Nathalie.

-No one that I noticed. I had my own concerns at the time and I was anxious to get into the city and checked into a hotel for the night. But, Tommy's mother did tell me a very strange tale. The little boy was having nightmares about a man.

Grace Stone interrupted.

-She did, Mr. Mendez. Sergeant? Tommy said he saw a man turn into a monster and, then, into a woman.

Debbie started crying.

-Yes. I didn't really see Tommy's monster; but, I did see a woman who kept staring at us when we were on the platform waiting for the train to pull in. She gave me the creeps.

Sgt. Rayno asked his next question.

-Debbie, can you describe this woman? Take your time.

-She looked hard and severe. Her hair was cut short and brushed straight back. Her face was so pale...like chalk.

-How was she dressed?

-I think- Yes! She had on a man's coat and pants.

Sgt. Rayno nodded to Edward. The P. I. picked up his colleague's cue.

-Any outstanding features, Debbie? Anything that might help us?

-No. It was so dark and it was starting to snow...and it was freezing cold. And, we were all pretty anxious to get home.

Sgt. Rayno turned back to Nathalie.

-Miss Montaigne? The description that Debbie just gave; does it jive with your own memory.

-I don't understand.

-The man who you saw kill Tommy Burton this morning; is there any similarity? Could it have been the same man? What exactly did you see?

Nathalie took another sip of water, much to Edward's annoyance. He wanted to shove the glass down her throat. Sgt. Rayno was having similar thoughts.

-Miss Montaigne? Stalling for time? I asked you a question.

She put down the glass of water.

-No. I saw a clean shaven man of indeterminate age. He could have been twenty-one or forty. Hard to tell. He was not tall. I am a good judge of height. I would place his height at five foot six or seven, no more. He moved...how shall I put it?

Sgt. Rayno prompted her.

-Go on, Miss Montaigne. I don't want to put words in your mouth.

-His movements were athletic like that of some cat burglar. His complexion was pale. At least, what I could see of his face. His coat collar was pulled up. And, his feet were quite small. Does that observation amuse you, Sergeant?

-No. And, I think we're about done here.

He looked at Edward.

-Mr. Mendez?

-Just a general question for Debbie.

Edward put out his cigarette and turned to face the pretty girl. Too bad she was so young.

-Debbie, I know this is hard for you.

-I'm okay, Mr. Mendez. Please...if it will help find my little cousin's killer.

-Did Tommy ever speak to you about the man he saw at the train station that night?

For a moment, Debbie stared past Nathalie.

-He did. He said the woman looked like a mannequin in a store window..

Edward raised an eyebrow.

-Did Tommy actually use that word, "mannequin."

-No. He said it was like one of those frozen ladies in the department store, but not as pretty.

Edward nodded to Sgt. Rayno that he was done. Sgt. Rayno called for a squad car to drive the three ladies home with a pointed warning to Nathalie Montaigne not to leave town. She assured them that she wouldn't.

The P. I. and the police officer were now alone in the interrogation room. Miss Raymond had also gone and was now busy transcribing her notes. .

-Don't worry, Eddie, we'll keep an eye on that French broad. I almost didn't recognize her. Man! She's aged about twenty years in the space of a few months.

-Her beady eyes gave her away. She's the type that never lets on to everything she knows. Plays her cards close to her flat chest.

-Wouldn't trust her from here to the damned door. Just don't like her.

-That makes two of us, Tom. She's a treacherous bitch; but, her being an eye witness today puts her life in danger. And, she knows that. And, she's plenty scared,.

-I'll say. We'll keep all three of them under police protection. So, what are your thoughts, shamus?

Sgt. Rayno put his feet up on the table. Edward did likewise and lit a cigarette.

-We're looking for a woman or a man disguised as one.

It was late evening and Lt. Donovan found himself standing outside the Intensive Care Unit at Mt. Sinai hospital on the upper east side of Manhattan. He tried looking through the glass "peep holes" of the double doors; but, all he could see were medical apparatus and a nurse standing over some kind of machine that looked like a life support unit.

Lt. William Donovan was worried. Only eight months ago the city had been plagued by two serial killers…both of them inhuman. Rotting corpses had been found throughout the city. The serial killers were caught and both were dead. The rotting corpses were incinerated for fear of contamination. The crisis was over…or was it? That's the question that was going through the Lieutenant's mind since 9 A.M. when he arrived at his precinct headquarters. One of his contacts out in Floral Park, Long Island sent him a coded message through the teletype: it signaled a case of extreme interest: one that should be looked into immediately. He telephoned his contact and what he heard was disturbing.

Was it starting all over again? Was another monster on the loose in the city? As soon as he could, he left for the hospital just before Sgt. Rayno got the call from Grand Central Station about the Tommy Burton murder.

A young girl walked by. He looked up and recognized her.

-Henriette Miller. How are you? Remember me?

-Yes? Oh, Lt. Donovan. I almost passed you by. How are you? And, of course I remember you.

-I've been better; but, for me, that's fine.

-And, what are you doing here, if I may ask? On a case or visiting a sick friend?

He smiled.

-I'm not visiting a friend, I can tell you that. Two patients were admitted five days ago: a married couple. The husband was D.O.A., but the wife is on life support and dangling by a thread, I'm told.

-I'm so sorry to hear that. Were they in some kind of automobile accident?

-No. Nothing like that. And, don't be sorry for me. I don't know them. But-

-Yes? Please, go on.

-I shouldn't be telling you any of this. It's a case I'm investigating. It could be serious.

-You look worried.

-I am. But, Miss Miller-

-Henriette, please.

-Henriette.

Lt. Donovan felt the blood rushing to his face.

-Henriette, what are you doing here? I thought you worked at the United Nations.

-I still do. But, I'm studying to be a nurse and I often visit the hospital and do volunteer work when I can.

-That's right. Now, I remember. You're a night student at Hunter studying nursing. You were a friend of Eva Ceres.

-Yes. And, she's never been found. I suppose-

-It's officially a cold case as far as Eva is concerned; but, the file is still open on my desk. We can at least try and locate her remains.

The swing door to the I.C.U. opened and Dr. Richard Aster approached Lt. Donovan. Dr. Aster reminded Lt. Donovan of some mad scientist from a Hollywood B movie. The doctor's salt and pepper hair was too long and uncombed. And, the look in his eye was either that of some wild savage or a man on the brink of a monumental discovery.

-Lt. Donovan? Sorry to keep you waiting so long; but, I had to do a double check on Mrs. Mills' vitals. A very strange and baffling case.

-Don't worry about it, Doctor. How's Mrs. Mills doing?

The Lieutenant introduced Henriette to the doctor.

-May I speak in front of Miss Miller?

-You bet. She's trustworthy.

Henriette blushed, but was quite flattered by the compliment.

-Good enough. Erica Mills is on the point of death. And, the cause of death will be attributed to advanced old age, if you can believe it.

-Just how old is she? I was told she was a young woman just recently married.

-She's twenty-three.

Henriette spoke up.

-I don't understand. How could a woman of twenty-three be dying of old age?

-An excellent question, Miss Miller. The only parallel that comes to mind is a disease called Hutchinson-Gifford syndrome.

-Yes. I have read about that in one of my medical textbooks at school. It's very rare and fatal. A young boy in Finland just recently died from the disease. He was only eleven years old.

Dr. Aster confirmed Henriette's statement and continued.

-Yes. I've read about that case, too. It's rare all right. I mean *really* rare. I've never seen it myself...well, just once in medical school and it was post-mortem. It's so rare that we really can't do any viable research on it.

Lt. Donovan broke in.

-Is that what Mrs. Mills has, Doctor? Some kind of aging disease...what you just said?

-It looks similar but, yet, markedly different. There's no distention of the forehead and it's pretty rare for anyone with Hutchinson-Gifford to live past the age of thirteen. The disease usually manifests at around age two. It doesn't seem to be hereditary. It appears in the family with no warning of a pre-history.

Dr. Aster shook his head.

-Mrs. Mills is not suffering from HG; but, she is dying of old age.

-Can I talk to her?

-It wouldn't do any good. We've got her on a respirator; but, we think that senility's set in.

-My God! What about her husband? What did the autopsy report say?

Dr. Aster again shook his head and sent his unruly hair flying in all directions.

-Inconclusive. An onset of a dozen ailments connected with old age: severe arthritis, heart failure, kidney failure, a collapsed lung — a general deterioration. I'll have the medics send you the report. It's quite an eyeful.

Dr. Aster took a deep breath.

-And, this from a young man who was vibrant and in peak condition not one week ago. His friend, George Sanderson, verified that. They were tennis partners at their country club and both men attended Harvard.

Lt. Donovan braced himself for his next question

-Is his corpse rotting, Doctor?

Dr. Aster looked at the Lieutenant as if he were quite mad.

-Rotting, did you say? You mean is it in a state of decay?

-You could put it that way.

-No. The aging process stopped upon death. Why do you ask, Lieutenant?

-Forget I asked it. Could I see Mrs. Mills now?

-All right. But, only for a few minutes. And, don't expect too much.

Lt. Donovan turned to Henriette.

-Wanna' come along? Might be good practice for you.

-Of course. If I would not be in the way.

The three people entered the I.C.U. Dr. Aster led them down a corridor and then into an area just to their right where Mrs. Mills was. Henriette gasped and Lt. Donovan did a double take. An emaciated old woman lay dying on a life support unit. Her mouth was wide open and her eyes stared vacantly into space. She was weak to the point where she was incapable of any voluntary movement. The nurse in attendance looked concerned. She spoke to the three who had just entered.

-Mrs. Mills is very weak. She hasn't much longer to live, poor thing.

Chapter Three
Thursday Evening, September 2, 1948
Trapped In A Web

JACK MARINO was sitting in his mother's living room. It was lit with only two small end table lamps. He was sitting next to his mother on her sofa. To meet Mrs. Marino was never to forget her. She dressed in bright colors like a gypsy. Her face was heavily made-up and her hair piled up in a "Madame Pompadour" way. She wore at least one ring on each finger and a half a dozen necklaces at any one time. Mrs. Marino also wore silver hoop earrings for psychic protection and insight into realms unseen and best unknown. She was also short and dumpy and spoke with an ever earnest voice of doom.

Maria Marino was a woman who lived on the edge of society. It was not the life she would have chosen; but, it's what her temperament and beliefs had forced her to adapt and make the best of. She attended meetings of the Theosophical Society and various other occult and fringe groups. She made friends easily, but not of long duration. People tended to use her and take advantage of her basic good nature. And, Mrs. Marino was not a stupid woman. She was well aware of people's motives and would usually cut off the relationship before any real damage was done.

However, at one such meeting she met a man who intrigued her: an Asian man who held himself aloof. To her surprise, this man engaged her in conversation. And, to Maria's surprise, she invited him to her home for dinner. He accepted. She was thrilled and worried: thrilled at the attentions of this man and worried about what he would think of her circumstances. Her apartment was small and she was not the neatest of housekeepers. As a matter of fact, she hated housework. But, on this special day, she made the effort to clean up and even went so far as to buy a new table cloth.

Mrs. Marino was entertaining two men that evening: her son, Jack, and this Asian man. The dinner had been a success with her guest complimenting her on every dish and the simplicity and yet beauty of her home. He was a man by the name of Mr. Kenneth Ng who was an extraordinarily handsome man in an expensive and well tailored suit. His eyes were dark and smoldering with traces of cruelty. He was the man who Jack had taken to the tenth floor that same afternoon. The man who had been knocking on Edward Mendez's office door. The man who had interrogated Jack not so long ago.

Mrs. Marino doted on her guest.

-Kenneth, my dear, another drink?

-Please and, then, I should go.

Jack felt ill at ease with this man who he immediately recognized, but who made no sign of recognition that he knew Jack. But, the young elevator operator retained his power of speech and good manners. When Mr. Ng drew out a cigarette from his silver case, he offered his mother's guest a light.

-Thank you.

-You're welcome.

-Tell me, Mr. Marino, does your life hold interest for you?

-Not especially, but-

-Yes?

-You wouldn't be interested.

-Try me.

-My weekend was... I really don't want to talk about it.

-There are bruises on your face. Were you mistreated by certain people?

-Part of my misadventure.

-May I offer you assistance?

-I can always use help. My future isn't exactly set in Roman concrete.

-No one's future is "exactly set;" but, the path that we follow is pre-ordained.

-I didn't know that. Not too sure I believe it.

-You should.

-Why?

-So, that you may alter it. Is that your wish?

-Could be.

-Can you help my son, Kenneth? Life is very hard for him.

-Your answer, Mr. Marino?

-Yes.

-If your life is to change, you must change your cir-cumstances. Are you willing to undertake that task?

-With all due respect, sir, why the interest in me?

-You remind me of someone: a young man back in Mexico. He also accepted my help.

-Who was he?

-You would not believe it if I were to tell you.

Jack smiled.

-I just might fool you, Mr. Ng.

-It involves the vague and often tangled concepts of reincarnation. The young man, Mr. Marino, was you.

Jack laughed.

-You're right. I don't believe it. I'm sorry. I don't mean to be rude.

Mrs. Marino spoke up.

-But, I do believe it. Mr. Ng, before you came, I read the tea leaves for my son. He hasn't long to live; but, yet, immortality is his for the choosing.

-I know of the immortality that you speak of, Mrs. Marino. It's the heaviest of burdens.

Mr. Ng addressed Jack.

-If you want to live, you must agree to an alteration.

-I'm not following you.

-You will soon be murdered for knowledge that you do not possess. Have you been followed?

-Maybe. This gray van keeps turning up. Kinda' hard not to notice it. You wouldn't know anything about it, would you?

Mr. Kenneth Ng would not openly admit in front of Jack's mother that he and her son had met that weekend.

-I know of this vehicle. It's a sign that your death warrant has been issued.

Mrs. Marino took a deep breath.

-Kenneth, what is this gray van? Who drives it?

-It's best that you don't know. As of yet, they offer no immediate threat, I believe.

Mrs. Marino pressed the matter.

-But, you're not sure about that, are you?

-No. I'm not certain.

Jack was about to excuse himself when Mr. Ng spoke.

-Mr. Marino, may I give you a lift?

-I can take the subway.

-It's late and I can offer you safe passage.

-Why not?

Kenneth Ng maneuvered his car through the light traffic of Manhattan's upper east side. His car had just been purchased and had all the latest accoutrements: radio, heater and even a built-in cigarette lighter. Jack Marino was admiring the car and appreciating the money that had purchased it.

-Nice car you got here, Mr. Ng.

-You appreciate good things. Perhaps, one day, you can afford the luxuries of life.

-That's a pipe dream for me. And, how come you pretended not to know me in front of my mother?

-The concealment was mutual.

-What did you take from Mr. Mendez's office?

-You must learn to mind your own business. Look over to your left. Do you see that man?

-What about him?

-If I ordered you to kill him, would you?

-You've gotta' be kidding. I'm no murderer. And, I don't like this kind of talk.

-Get used to it, young man. There's a parking space up ahead. We will overtake that man and then waylay him. I can see no witnesses about.

-No. I'm not gonna' do this. Let me out of this car.

-It's too late for you. Here. We've arrived.

Mr. Ng. parked his car and got out. He walked in the direction of the man he had pointed out to Jack. He stopped the man to ask a question. The man looked puzzled. Mr. Ng took out a knife and thrust it through the man's heart. The victim fell to the pavement…dead.

Jack got out of the car and ran over to the fallen man.

-Why did you do that?

-Never mind the sanctimonious concern. Get back in the car and we'll be on our way. I've a few things to say to you, young man.

-You're not getting me back in that car. Forget it!

-You will do as you're told. Now, before it's too late, we must leave the scene of the crime. A senseless murder, yes, but a necessary one for you.

Mr. Ng walked back to his car followed by a reluctant and bewildered Jack Marino.

And, once back on the road and away from the corpse…

-You are now an accessory to a murder. You are also a homosexual man who has had an assignation with a military man back in the state of Maryland. Your crimes are mounting.

-I'm no accessory. What's to stop me from going straight to the cops?

-I will deny everything. And, the weapon is in your coat pocket. I conveniently placed it there as you were whining about that man's life.

Jack reached into his coat pocket and threw the knife out the car window.

-That was very stupid of you. Your fingerprints are on the weapon. And, that man's wallet is missing because you stole it.

-I didn't!

-You did. I saw you. What you did with it, I've no idea.

-What are you doing to me?

-Making certain that you will help us when you are called upon. I left an envelope at your mother's house with the sum of five thousand dollars in it. She will, of course, share it with her son.

-Leave my mother out of this.

-Her safety and yours will be dependent on your reliability.

Jack sat back in his seat. He knew he was defeated.

Mr. Ng stopped for a red light and looked over at Jack.

-Don't be so dejected. You are now on the fringe of our group; but one day soon you will be — how shall I put it? — a full fledged member. You will be where I am now…and a victim of your own will be seated next to you.

Marlena Lake entered her living room to be greeted by Isolde Himmel.

-Marlena. I'll fix you a drink.

-The usual: bourbon and water.

-Of course.

Marlena sat down in her usual armchair watching her guest's every movement.

-Miss Himmel, we haven't seen very much of you, lately. What have you been up to?

-Research and-

-Yes?

-I may be leaving for Europe very soon.

-Whereabouts and when?

-Germany, I think. I can't give you an exact date; but, you'll be the first to know.

-Why Germany, Miss Himmel? You don't mind that I call you by your feminine counterpart?

-Not at all. It simplifies the masquerade. It's what I usually present to the public at large. I forgot your question.

-Why Germany? It's far from being rebuilt.

-Exactly. Its chaos is what attracts me to it.

-And, I thought you such an ordered person.

-Perhaps, not so ordered as you thought.

-Miss Himmel, your knowledge of ancient Sumer has proven invaluable to my research into that ancient and mysterious culture. I'll be sorry to see you leave. And, your first-hand knowledge of ancient Rome is staggering. Why haven't you written about it yourself?

-Here's your drink. And, you make me feel quite humble. And, I do have one last favor to ask of you.

-Pray tell?

-A séance. I'd like to hold one.

Marlena took a sip of her drink.

-I don't like seances. They open portals to God-only-knows-where. One is never entirely in control.

-I'm not overly fond of them myself. And, of course, I would not hold it here in your home. An associate of mine would preside at her residence.

-Then, where?

-At her apartment here in the city.

-Why?

-Her apartment is on the 23rd floor and the vista from it is clear of any obstructions.

-I see. Freshen my drink, will you?

-Of course.

-Miss Himmel, what is the purpose of this séance?

-To test an invited guest's mettle, if you would. With your permission, we'll send out the invitations in your name.

-Why not in your friend's name?

-He will be more familiar with your name, Marlena. And, I might as well tell you, you are already acquainted with my associate.

-Her name?

-Miss Linda Kawano.

-Yes. I know her. A rather enigmatic person.

Miss Himmel smiled.

-Enigmatic and cruel. Her heart is as cold and empty as the vacuum of space.,

Chapter Four

Thursday Night, September 2, 1948
The Night Owl

EDWARD HUNG up the phone on an irate Yolanda Estravades. All day long she had waited for him and now he had to cancel their dinner date. He would drop by later and just maybe she'd fix him something to eat?

He sat back down and took out a cigarette. Lt. Donovan had just briefed him and Sgt. Rayno on the Mills' case: husband dead and wife dying of premature old age.

Edward shook his head and took a puff on his cigarette.

-But, no rotting corpses? I hope.

-That was my thought, too, Mendez. No. Not this time. Thank God for small favors. And, this just might be an isolated case. At least, that's what we're hoping for.

Sgt. Rayno blew Edward's cigarette smoke back.

-But, how'd they catch it? Whatever the hell "it" is. Eddie, you look kinda' worried.

-This couple lived out in Long Island?

-Someplace in Stuart Manor.

-That's not too far out. Never been there myself. Who found them?

-A married couple by the name of Sanderson.

-Have they been questioned?

-Not by me. You want to have a look into it, Mendez?

-As a matter of fact, I would. Did you get the autopsy report, yet, on the husband?

-It's on its way. Mendez, what is it, man? You look real deep in thought. You got a lead you want to share with us?

-You wouldn't have any recent newspapers around, would you? Something's ticking in the back of my head.

Sgt. Rayno got up.

-I'll scout around for some. Got a date you can give me?

-Try this past Tuesday or Wednesday, Tom. And, thanks.

-Don't mention it. It's what they pay me for.

That left Lt. Donovan and Edward alone in the interrogation room: two men who were not the best of friends.

-Well, Mendez, looks like you've got two cases on your hands. Think you can handle it?

-Won't be the first time, that is, if they are two cases. That good ole' P. I. gut feeling is kicking around in this thick head.

-You mean there's a connection between the Grand Central Station murder and this "old age" thing? I don't see it,

-I wouldn't go that far just yet. I gotta' talk to a few people first.

-Clue me in.

-Tommy's mother for one and that Sanderson couple out in Long Island.

-Better go easy with the kid's mother. I hear she lost her husband not too long ago.

Sgt. Rayno came back in flipping through a newspaper.

-Here you go, Eddie. You can take 'em with you if you like. I got Tuesday's and Wednesday's edition of The Night Owl.

-Thanks a lot, Tom. I'll bring 'em back.

The P. I. put on his Fedora.

-And, now I gotta' buy me some flowers for my girlfriend.

As soon as Edward left the interrogation room, Lt. Donovan went back to his office on that same floor. He closed the glass panel behind him and sat down at his desk. He wanted to reach for the Dolores Sarney file: a case that had so far gone unsolved. The Lieutenant had been on the police force too long to not know when someone was holding out on him. Dolores Sarney was killed like a pig being slaughtered: gutted and thrown into the river. It was a crime that Lt. Donovan couldn't let go of. He knew that Mendez and his girlfriend were involved up to their necks…and so was that pompous ass, Marlena Lake. One of them would have to crack…but which one. Maybe…just maybe Miss Lake's daughter, Susan, would be the weak link in the chain.

Lt. Donovan lit a cigarette and sat back. Yes. Keep your friends real close and keep those enemies a lot closer...even if you hate their stinking guts. And, maybe...just maybe, he could get them on another crime? Could he do it alone? No. He'd need help, but not from Sgt. Rayno. The Sergeant and Mendez had become friends. The Lieutenant would have to do likewise, even if it killed him.

-That was a great meal, baby. It hit the spot.

-I know that you work hard, Edward. I didn't mean to be angry with you before on the phone; but, I had a hard time at practice today and the new artistic program isn't working out. We might have to change the music.

-I can't wait to see the run-through.

Edward plopped himself down on the sofa.

-Come here and sit next to me.

-Let me finish these dishes first. Talk to me.

-You'll never guess who I ran in to today.

-Then, you'd better tell me. I'm not so good at guessing games.

-You better put that dish down first. Don't wanna' break it.

Yolanda smiled and placed the dish into the rack to dry.

-Okay. I'm ready.

-None other than Nathalie Montaigne.

-Oh, my God! You mean that woman had the nerve to show herself?

Yolanda sat down next to Edward on the sofa.

-Where did you meet her? Was she arrested, finally?

Edward put his arm around his girlfriend and laughed.

-You're not too far off. She's actually a key witness to a murder you'll be reading about in tomorrow's paper. I almost didn't recognize her.

-Oh? Was she wearing some kind of disguise?

-Just the opposite. The heavy make-up was all gone and so was that fake looking wig of hers.

Yolanda smiled.

-I'm surprised that you recognized her at all. I'll bet she looked every bit her age.

-And, then some.

The P. I. gave his girlfriend a full account of young Tommy's murder and his meeting with Sgt. Rayno and Lt. Donovan. He looked around for a cigarette and spotted his pack of Lucky Strikes on the end table.

-Want one?

-No. Thanks.

-You're awfully quiet. Is it about little Tommy?

-So terrible to kill a young boy; but, it's something else, too. I was thinking about that couple out in Long Island and that strange disease.

Edward grinned.

-I shouldn't have told you about that. That, you won't be reading about in tomorrow's paper. They're keeping it under wraps until the medics can start to make heads or tails out of it.

Yolanda looked at her boyfriend, surprised.

-But, Edward, I have read about it. Not about that couple, but about this woman in Brooklyn who died this past Sunday.

He took in that statement.

-That's kind of what I said to Tom. It's in the back of my head, somewhere, that I've read about this or at least glanced at the headline. You wouldn't still have that paper, baby?

-No. I threw it out. I never keep them.

-That's okay. Let me get up. I brought a couple of papers home with me from the precinct.

Edward went over to the coat stand by the door and reached up to get the newspapers. He brought them over to Yolanda and handed her one.

-It was in the Night Owl edition, right? Say yes.

-It had to be. It's the only edition that I get.

-Good. Start looking, baby.

The two of them started flipping through the pages of the N.Y. Daily News' Night Owl edition. It didn't take them long to find that particular article.

-Edward! Here it is.

-Let's read it together.

"Brooklyn resident, Missy Wingate, arrived D.O.A. at Wyckoff General Hospital this Sunday evening. The cause of death was congestive heart failure among other non-life threatening ailments. Miss Wingate's age was listed as twenty-four; but, if that were the case, she was the oldest twenty-four year old woman on record. An autopsy was performed by Dr. Claire Ingram and Miss

Wingate's age was determined at approximately ninety years.

"The birth certificate obtained from city records was clearly indicative of another woman with a similar surname. "Missy" being an obvious nickname of sorts. Ninety years ago, birth certificates were not as common or readily available as they are today.

"A case of mistaken identity? Not according to her friend, Patty Kilmeade, who swears her friend was a healthy, if overweight, woman of twenty-four. No relatives have come forward to claim the body. No further investigation is underway."

Yolanda and Edward were silent for a few minutes. Somehow, that news article didn't make too much sense.

-Edward?

-Uh-huh?

-Why no further investigation? That woman, Patty Kilmeade, should know how old her friend was, shouldn't she?

-I'd say, yes. But, the cops probably think she's some kind of kook or just someone who wants to get her name in the papers.

-But, this Missy Wingate must have had other friends. Couldn't they verify Patty's story?

Edward smiled.

-You two on a first name basis? The cops probably don't think it's worth their time. The woman died of a heart attack and the autopsy verifies that. The chick was overweight and overweight people are more prone to drop dead of heart attacks.

-Are you really buying that, Edward?

-No. I want to take a look at that autopsy report and question this Patty Kilmeade whose name rings a distant bell in this P. I.'s head.

After some good sex, Edward lay naked on top of the bed sheets deep in thought and quite satisfied. The night air was chilly but it helped keep his mind alert and focused. He had a lot on his shamus' plate.

-Tomorrow's Friday, so I better get down to Wyckoff Hospital and route out that autopsy report along with the doctor who performed it. And, then, it's on to Patty Kilmeade which oughta' be just as interesting.

Edward reached over for his pack of cigarettes on the night table.

-Saturday, a few more interviews: Nathalie Montaigne is on the top of that list, Tommy's mother and even Mrs. Stone and Debbie. Tom is going to head over to the Sandersons to see if they can shed any light.

The phone rang and Edward nearly jumped out of his skin. Yolanda stirred and turned over in her sleep. She was a sound sleeper. He picked up the receiver.

-Edward Mendez.

-Eddie? It's Tom Rayno. Sorry to wake you, man.

-What's up? And, I know it's gotta' be real bad news.

-Real bad. Real interesting. The Sandersons were found murdered execution style.

-What the hell...

-Yup. A bullet through the head on each of them. The neighbors heard gunshots around 11 P.M., but thought it might just be the Sanderson's TV set. They've got one, you know. A couple of teenagers were coming back from a movie and spotted the front door open.

-Wide open? That was pretty careless or arrogant.

-You know what we say on the force: most criminals are just plain stupid.

-If you're looking for an argument, don't.

-The wire came in a few minutes ago. I was catching up on some paper work.

-Is Donovan there?

-No. He went home, I think. Tried ringing him up and got no answer.

Edward put out his cigarette.

-A bullet through the head for little Tommy Burton and now the Sandersons. Why? God-damn-it. Why? And this aging business on top of it all.

He related the news article to Sgt. Rayno.

-You figure this Wingate gal really did die of some old age disease like John Mills?

-It's out in left field; but, I think it's worth checking out. How's Erica Mills doing? Is she still breathing?

-As far as I know, she's still alive, barely.

-I've got me a full plate for tomorrow, Tom. Think you can take a look in on Erica Mills – like real early? Sometimes people rally at the last minute before kicking off.

-First thing, man. Even if I have to push my way in. Where you heading for?

-Patty Kilmeade. Hey, Tom, have you got a phone book for Brooklyn in arm's reach?

-I sure do. Hold on.

Edward lit another cigarette and waited.

-Hey, Eddie, this Patty Kilmeade owns a bakery out in Bensonhurst called "Patty's Cakes."

Edward snapped his fingers.

-I knew that name was familiar! My sisters go there once in a long while. I've been there myself a couple of times way back when. Thanks, Tom, and keep in touch.

Chapter Five

Friday, September 3, 1948
Murder at the Bakery

EDWARD DROVE his Ford into Brooklyn. It was another beautiful September day: sunny and brisk and a person needed to wear a jacket or sweater to keep out the pre-autumn chill. He was wearing his navy suit with a light sweater underneath his suit jacket. He turned on to 86th St. and found a parking space just across from "Patty's Cakes." He got out of his car, locked up and crossed the street. The bakery was just opening up as the P. I. walked in. There were no customers just yet. Good. There wouldn't be any interruptions or distractions. Edward saw the owner and one of her helpers behind the glass counter getting ready for business. He took off his Fedora and tried not to look at all the delicious baked goods: pastries, cookies, pies, cup cakes….but the aroma of the delicacies was getting to him.

-Patty Kilmeade?

-That's me, handsome. How can I help you?

-Edward Mendez: Private Investigator.

-Oh, I know your sisters. Your sister, Dottie, was here just last Sunday. and we had a nice chat.

She stopped short, catching her breath.

-You're a police detective, right?

-I'm not on the police force; but, I do work with them on cases. Can we talk about last Sunday?

-You mean about poor Missy, don't you?

-About Missy's death.

Edward could see that the woman was on the verge of tears.

-Maybe, we could sit at that table over there in the corner? I'll buy us both a cup of your great coffee. My sisters can't praise it enough.

-You bet. Toni can handle the counter. She knows the store better than I do. Just give me a second and I'll bring over the coffee.

Edward made himself comfortable and took a good look around the place: neat and clean with wrought iron chairs and glass topped tables and sparkling white floor. He caught sight of the dangling golden dispenser that contained the string for tying boxes of pastries, cookies and cakes. It used to fascinate him when he was a little boy.

-Here you go, hon'. It's a French blend I'm trying out. I hope you like it.

The patroness sat down opposite the P. I. Edward noticed the weariness around the women's gray eyes and the lines around the mouth.

-Patty, how well did you know Missy Wingate?

-It'd have to be close to four years. She used to come in on Sunday afternoons for coffee and crumb cake. It was always crumb cake, that was her favorite. She'd have two slices, but she was trying to cut back.

-What kind of person was she?

-She was kind of the shy type, but you wouldn't think it to look at her. Me? I'm more outgoing. I wore down her little defenses and we got to be good friends; almost confidantes, if you know what I mean.

Edward smiled.

-I think so. Did she have a family? Did she have many friends...*any* friends besides you?

-I know that her parents died when she was a teenager just out of high school. I don't know what of. And, she never mentioned any relatives. And, I don't think she had many friends. Missy was very self conscious about her weight, a lot more than she let on. Always dieting and going to exercise classes that didn't really do any good. Oh, I shouldn't say that. It's not nice.

-What did she do for fun?

-She liked strolling on the boardwalk at Coney Island, even in the winter time. She liked looking at the ocean and the seagulls. I think she even collected sea shells.

-I kind of like that myself. Good coffee, by the way.

-Oh, thanks, hon'.

-Patty, last Sunday, how was she feeling? Did she look ill?

Patty was about to burst into tears.

-Oh, Mr. Mendez-

-Edward. And, take your time. Try some of your great coffee, it'll make you feel better.

Patty took a few sips of the coffee.

-Oh, it is good. Edward. She looked just awful! I almost didn't recognize her. She looked so old and withered. I couldn't imagine what happened to her. It just wasn't normal. She was only twenty-four for pity's sake.

He nodded, holding on to his white, porcelain coffee cup.

-Patty, are you sure it was Missy?

-Oh, for heaven sake! Of course I am. I recognized her clothes and her shoulder bag and even her gym sneakers. It was her for sure. Oh, Edward, when she came in, she practically collapsed into the chair you're sitting on. And, when I came back with the aspirin, she was on the floor. It was just too awful.

-And, she was definitely twenty-four?

Patty smiled at that question.

-Well...she might have fudged a couple of years; but, she couldn't have been more than thirty.

Patty leaned forward.

-Edward, when she came in, she looked ninety! It was like this big sack of jelly-

An explosion and glass shattering everywhere. Patty leaned to the side with half her head blown off. Her young assistant screamed hysterically. By sheer reflex, Edward squatted down just in time as another bullet barely missed him and instead shattered into the wall.

There was nothing left of the windows; shards of glass were all over the floor. Toni, the assistant, stopped screaming and was now sobbing behind the counter. Edward made his way over to the girl. He knew that

Patty was dead and beyond help. He made a leap to get behind the counter.

-Toni. Toni! Try and get a grip. Did you see who took a shot at us?

-No. Thank God! I just heard the explosion and covered my eyes. Is Patty hurt?

-Yes.

Edward peered over the counter. No one was in sight. He took out his gun and ran to the shattered door where he crouched down again and took aim.

-Toni? Is there a phone in the back?

-In the kitchen.

-Call the cops and stay back there out of sight. Make sure the back door's locked.

-Okay.

Edward got to his feet. A couple of passersby were staring at him and the shattered store front. Traffic on the road seemed normal enough: no sign of any getaway car.

Patty Kilmeade's killer had gotten away.

An hour later, Edward was placing a call from the corner phone booth.

-Hey, Tom?

-I know, Eddie.

-Christ! The cop grape vine, man. Einstein was wrong, some things can travel faster than the speed of light.

Sgt. Rayno laughed.

-You just might have something there.

Edward leaned against the phone booth's folding door.

-Anything on the Sandersons?

-Yup. A couple of odd things.

-Right up my alley. Let's hear it.

-Puncture mark behind their necks, right at the base of the brain stem, they tell me. Infected. Like someone stuck a dirty needle in them.

-So, they were drugged and then shot?

-Looks like it, but don't quote me on that.

-Doesn't make sense.

He lit a cigarette.

-Was there a puncture mark on the Mills' couple?

-There was. Some of your shamus' gut feeling must be rubbing off on me. As soon as I finished with the Sandersons, I ran a check on John Mills. The coroner noticed a puncture mark behind his neck, too.

-What about his wife?

-Lt. Donovan checked that one out. You can make that four puncture wounds.

-But, Erica Mills is still hanging in there.

-The chief is with her now. They think she's about to kick off; but, he's hoping she'll come to first.

-Better put an armed guard around her, Tom.

-Done. Eddie? What's your next move?

Edward exhaled a puff of smoke.

-Well, if they haven't taken Missy Wingate out of the morgue...

-Good luck, man. And, by the way, about the Sandersons...not only was the front door left open, but every light bulb in the house was busted.

Edward let out a long, low whistle.

-This gets more bizarre by the minute. Tom? I'll try and hook up with you later.

Edward Mendez gave his statement to the police along with young Toni, whose parents came to take her home. He left the phone booth and got into his Ford. The drive to Wyckoff Hospital wasn't that far and it would give the P. I. time to think.

Patty Kilmeade was a credible witness as far as Edward was concerned. He'd been impressed with her demeanor and sincerity. A damn shame she was murdered. And that meant one thing: she had either seen something she shouldn't have or someone was afraid that Missy Wingate had confided in her friend something incriminating and wasn't taking any chances.

So what the hell had happened to Missy Wingate? How long had she been ill and how did she contract this pretty horrible disease – if it was a disease – through a dirty needle...what in hell was in that needle?

Edward was now face-to-face with the physician who had performed the autopsy on the late Missy Wingate. She was a petite woman with a mane of black hair who wore thick glasses that somehow suited her; a beauty, she wasn't, but Edward got the impression that she could care less. Very business-like, bordering on brusque.

-Well, Mendez, what can I do for you?

-Is Missy Wingate's body still here?

-It is. Want to see it?

-Yes, Doctor…

He couldn't remember the name from the newspaper article.

-Doctor Claire Ingram. This way.

Edward dutifully followed. And, in another minute, they stopped in front of file 393.

-The late Miss Wingate: not a pretty sight.

Doctor Ingram slid the tray out of its compartment and uncovered the face of the deceased.

-Doctor, how old would you say this woman was?

-Ninety, if she's a day.

Edward shook his head.

-She sure as hell looks it. There's nothing to indicate that she was younger?

-How do you mean, Mendez?

-Missy Wingate was twenty-four...thirty, at most.

Dr. Ingram let out a brief but demonstrative laugh.

-Surely, you jest. This woman was well into her advanced years. She died of heart failure. And, given her height and weight, I'm surprised she made it to old age.

-Got ya'.

This was not the type of woman you argued with.

-Tell me, Doctor, were there any needle marks on her?

-You mean was she a dope addict?

-That's not what I meant, but it's a thought.

Dr. Ingram took her clip board and pointed at the cadaver's neck.

-There was evidence of a needle mark behind the neck at the base of the brain stem.

Bingo!

-Dr. Ingram?

-Yes, Mendez?

-This is gonna' sound off the wall, but is there any known drug that could bring on old age?

-Like a reverse fountain of youth? No. Illness, yes. I've seen it happen before.

-Would you consider old age an illness?

-Some would. I don't. It's a natural process of the human anatomy, like it or not. Most don't.

-You can slide her back in, Doctor.

With a thud and a click, Missy Wingate was back in the deep freeze.

Edward reached for a cigarette, but didn't light it.

-Missy Wingate had a friend with her when she died.

-Yes. The hysterical type, but harmless enough.

-That woman was murdered just a couple of hours ago. Her head was blown off.

-Sorry to hear it. And, the reason?

-She knew something, Doctor Ingram. And, I gotta' find out what it was.

Edward was about to leave, but changed his mind.

-Doctor Ingram?

-Yes?

-A young- well, old woman is now dying of old age. When she was brought in, she was listed as twenty-three. The medics now list her as ninety-seven.

-And, she's alive?

-You could call it that.

Did nothing shock this woman?

-Where is she being treated?

-At Mt. Sinai, if she's not already dead. Her husband *is* dead of old age. He was twenty-four.

Dr. Ingram stared long and hard at Mendez and his unlit cigarette.

-Are you heading into the city, Mendez?

-If you want a ride, I'll give you a lift.

-Please. Give me five minutes to check out and speak to my assistant. Don't go away. And, save a cigarette for me. I'm all out.

The I.C.U. was crowded with one too many visitors and physicians. Doctors Richard Aster and Claire Ingram, Edward Mendez, Sgt. Rayno, and Lt. Donovan. At this particular moment, Dr. Ingram was bending over Erica Mills and examining her eyes.

-Interesting.

-What is it, Doctor?

Dr. Ingram straightened up and addressed Dr. Aster.

-This woman is blind; but, I can't detect any discernible cause.

-Aside from old age, you mean?

-Quite. And, Doctor, take a look at her neck. That puncture mark is quite wide. It's almost like some kind of wound.

-I've noted that. A dirty syringe? An insect bite?

-I'd hate to meet that insect. Let's see if she's lucid, shall we?

-You'd better hurry, Doctor Ingram. I don't think my patient has much time left.

Edward, Sgt. Rayno, and Lt. Donovan were listening intently to this medical discussion.

Dr. Ingram bent over to speak to Erica Mills. Gently, she touched the patient's arm.

-Mrs. Mills? I'm Dr. Claire Ingram. We're trying to help you; but, we need your help in doing so. Can you hear me, dear?

Erica Mills blinked her sightless eyes. Dr. Claire Ingram's next question shocked everyone.

-Who did this to you?

The look of terror in Mrs. Mills' eyes was unmistakable.

-Did someone inject you with a syringe? Someone did this to you.

The barest of whispers was heard.

-The shadow...I didn't see it...a prank...a phantom.

Doctor Ingram looked puzzled.

-A shadow, Mrs. Mills? Someone's idea of a practical joke? A prankster dressed up as a phantom?

-I'm dying... Where is John? Where is my husband? Is he all right?

Dr. Ingram evaded her question.

-We're doing everything we can for you, Mrs. Mills. Please, try and stay calm.

-The fun house. John was angry... I told him...

Mrs. Mills' body heaved as she went into cardiac arrest.

A half hour later out in the hospital corridor, the five people gathered. Lt. Donovan addressed the two physicians.

-How in hell does a twenty-three year old woman age seventy years in the space of one week and, then, drop dead? You got any answers for me, Doctors, 'cause I'm sure looking for some?

Doctor Ingram looked the Lieutenant square in the eye.

-She was injected with an age accelerant.

-What the hell is that?

-Her cellular structure went into overdrive. You do know, Lieutenant, that theoretically speaking we shouldn't age at all, but somehow we all manage it.

-Well, Doctor Ingram, Mrs. Mills sure as hell did – and then some!

Dr. Ingram addressed Dr. Aster.

-We'll need to do a complete blood and fluid analysis. And, hair and tissue samples, of course. And, that wound on her neck...I didn't like the look of that. It was obviously infected. Yes. Autopsies on all three victims. And, I'll have another look at Missy Wingate.

-I'll see to all the arrangements, Doctor Ingram.

Edward broke in.

-What did Mrs. Mills say to you?

-Something about a shadow or phantom in a fun house.

-"Fun house" like in amusement park?

-That's where they generally are. I've never found them very amusing or scary myself.

Edward continued.

-If Mrs. Mills was injected with something – and I heard you ask her that – then, we've got a double homicide on our hands. And, that's not counting Missy Wingate and Patty Kilmeade.

-Don't leave out the Sandersons.

That was Sgt. Rayno who looked over at Lt. Donovan.

-Lieutenant Donovan?

-I'm here, Sergeant. Get on the phone over there by the elevator and put in a call to HQ. I want round the clock protection for Debbie Stone. All of this is linked, somehow; but, I'll make bet that Miss Stone is the next target.

-You think there's a connection with little Tommy's murder?

-Yes, Sergeant, I do.

Lt. Donovan looked over at Edward, a man he still didn't completely trust.

-Mendez?

-So do I, Lieutenant. The bullet to the head of little Tommy and Mr. and Mrs. Sanderson: there's gotta' be a link: same execution style killings. They got sloppy with Patty Kilmeade: probably an awkward angle.

-Real awkward; but, pretty damned accurate or...a different hitman. We'll compare the bullets that killed little Tommy Burton and Patty Kilmeade. I'm betting that they'll match.

Chapter Six
Saturday, September 4, 1948
Interviews

IT WAS Saturday and Edward was parking his Ford in front of a warehouse that was across the street from Edith Burton's and Nathalie Montaigne's building. He got out, went across the street and rang Miss Montaigne's doorbell. It was answered immediately.

Edward climbed the two flights of stairs in the well lit but run down hallway. Nathalie stood in the open doorway waiting for him.

-Cherie, come in. I've been expecting you. Lovely day outside, no?

It was a rhetorical question so Edward didn't bother responding.

The P. I. entered the small and sparsely furnished apartment.

-Sit down on the love seat. I prefer the armchair over here.

Edward lit a cigarette and offered the Frenchwoman one which she accepted.

-Your Lucky Strikes are quite delicious. I remember smoking them in your car so many nights ago.

-Nathalie, I'm gonna' try and make this real brief.

-I have all day. Don't rush on my account. Life is quite boring for me, lately.

-About that December night last year at the train stop, you have told us everything you know? That's a question and a statement.

-On my father's grave, yes. I swear it.

Edward believed her.

-Were there any other witnesses? Can you recall anyone else in that waiting area?

-Yes. There was Eric Stone, Grace's son who is now at some military academy in Maryland, I believe. But, I spoke to the young man and he recalled only the train delay. He's not the observant type like his sister, Debbie.

-Lucky for him.

-Indeed. And-

-Go on.

-There was Debbie's friend who works in downtown Brooklyn. She was there, as well. But, I've never gotten the chance to speak to her.

-What's her name?

-Let me think. Teresa Farmer. She works in a place called McCrory's right near all the department stores. I dropped by for a knish one day – I had a craving – and to do some shopping; but the young girl was too busy to speak to me.

-Do you think this Teresa Farmer knows anything?

-I've no idea. But, Debbie tells me that she likes to gossip and that kind are always observant, no?

Edward put out his cigarette.

-Maybe. But what she saw just might kill her.

Someone was knocking on Nathalie Montaigne's door. She got up to answer it.

-It must be Edith. Mrs. Burton.

The mountain had come to Mohammed.

-Edith, please come in.

Mrs. Burton entered the apartment and started at seeing a stranger in the living room.

-I'm sorry. I didn't know you had company.

-No, my dear. It is quite all right. This is Mr. Edward Mendez and he is a private investigator. He's here to-

Mrs. Burton finished the statement.

-To find my little boy's murderer. I saw him come into the building.

-Please, cherie, sit down over here.

Edward gave the woman time to collect her thoughts and relax. He didn't want to rush her; but, he could see how grief stricken she was. It was Mrs. Burton who addressed the P. I.

-Mr. Mendez, do you know who killed my little Tommy?

-We have a lead on a suspect, Mrs. Burton. We'll find him. I promise you that.

-Why, Mr. Mendez? Why would anyone do this?

-Murderers are not rational people. They kill out of desperation and fear. They have no moral code.

Nathalie spoke up.

-They live on the fringes of society. Anger and resentment…that is what fuels most of them.

-Mrs. Burton? Did Tommy ever mention anyone specifically to you?

-I don't know what you mean.

-Did he name any individual who he was afraid of?

-No. Never a name. He only had nightmares about monsters and women who looked like mannequins. He was only a little boy with a vivid imagination.

-He saw two men on the station platform that December night. Did he hear them speak to each other? Nathalie...did you hear them say anything?

-I don't recall, cherie. I don't think so. We were all overcome by the attempted suicide.

Edward believed her.

-Mrs. Burton? Did Tommy every say anything about overhearing the two men speak to each other?

Mrs. Burton was quiet for a minute, trying to think.

-Yes. Yes, Mr. Mendez. Tommy did mention a name. He said one of the men told the other, "He did a good job of it, Joseph."

-Thank you, Mrs. Burton. You've been a big help. And, I'll be in touch.

Teresa Farmer was a young and attractive woman of nineteen. She graduated highschool a couple of years ago and went straight to work. Her mom worked in the same McCrory's store, but at the fast service food counter. Teresa's dad died just two years ago and mother and daughter had to fend for themselves. They didn't whine about it. They just did what had to be done and made the best of it.

Teresa was a pretty brunette with dark, brown eyes and a sharp sense of humor that was tempered by her warmth and good nature. Any relative or friend who came to her counter always got a frankfurter on a bun free of charge. Her younger relatives got treated to an ice cream cone. She didn't know that today might be her last day on earth.

Edward Mendez maneuvered his Ford through the downtown Brooklyn traffic. It was just about the same area where he learned how to drive. His eyes were on the heavy traffic: vehicular and pedestrian; but his attention was focused on one particular car: the car that was tailing him since he left the Presbyterian Hospital.

-The same bastard probably tailed me to Patty's bakery. I'm on to you, pal, and my gun is loaded. We'll see who's faster on the trigger.

It took the P. I. the better part of a half hour to find a parking space in the crowded shopping area; and, it was a narrow squeeze at that. He locked up and headed to McCrory's down the street. His tail was nowhere to be seen, but Edward knew enough not to relax his guard.

He walked into McCrory's and looked about for the girl that Nathalie had described to him. He spotted her serving an ice cream soda to a young woman. He didn't walk directly to the girl. His P. I. gut instinct told him that his presence put her in danger.

He made an irregular circuit about the main floor glancing at the variety of counters and displays. And, then he spotted him: tall and thin and wearing a dark trench coat. Was the bastard chewing gum? Edward stopped at a candy counter that had a full mirror display. His tail was getting careless. Edward had a full view of the man's face: pale and gaunt and...young? The P. I. couldn't be sure, but he looked like some punk kid.

Edward drew his Waltham out of its shoulder holster but kept it hidden under his suit jacket. He turned about and walked toward his pursuer who didn't move. As Edward drew nearer a crowd of woman customers came between them. When they finally passed, Edward's tail had vanished.

-Damn it! He's gotta' still be in the store someplace. He couldn't have gotten out that fast. He's gotta' still be on the main floor.

No sign of him. Cautiously, Edward made his way to the food counter and found himself an empty stool. He was facing another mirror so he could at least keep an eye out for the bastard.

-May I help you?

-Teresa Farmer?

-Yes.

-You don't know me, Miss Farmer. Edward Mendez, P. I. Here's my card.

-Oh. Are you investigating little Tommy's murder?

-I am. Miss Farmer, I'm going to stand up and I want you to stay directly in my sight. When I move, you will move with me. I'm going to guide you out of this store. Please, trust me.

The young girl was frightened, but some inner wisdom told her to trust his man.

-All right, Mr. Mendez.

-Good girl. Let's go.

-Miss, my check, please?

She ignored the customer. Edward and Teresa reached the edge of the long counter. Edward took the girl's hand and they started walking toward the exit.

A gunshot rang out; but Edward Mendez was ready. He pulled Teresa to the floor, got up on one knee and took aim. He saw his target but the panic stricken customers were blocking his aim.

The killer was on the loose.

-Teresa, get up. We're getting the hell out of here.

He pulled the frightened girl to her feet.

-Let's go.

Edward was hoping that under the cover of the fleeing customers would give the two of them enough camouflage to get out of the store with their lives intact. They made it to the exit when another shot rang out. And, by God's grace, no one was hit.

In another minute, the P. I. was pulling out of his parking space with Teresa Farmer sitting beside him.

-It's okay, Teresa. I'm taking you to Grace Stone's place. She and Debbie are under police protection. You'll be safe enough there.

She had been crying; but, now she wiped her eyes with a handkerchief and spoke with composure.

-Why? Why, Mr. Mendez? Was that Tommy's killer trying to kill me, too? What does he want?

-I'd make bet on it. And, maybe, you can tell me what he wants.

-I don't understand. Why me? Why Tommy? How could we be a threat to anyone?

-Teresa? I want you to think back – real hard, like – to a night back in December when the sun disappeared.

She knew what night the P. I. was talking about.

-When that man tried to kill himself? I remember it all right. Who could forget it?

-What do you remember? Tell it any way you want.

-I saw a man being brought out. He was supposed to be dead.

-He is now. Didn't mean to interrupt.

-And, two other men were with him. One was Egyptian looking and had one of those pencil mustaches. I didn't like his look, neither did Debbie.

Edward smiled. No one liked Turhan Aswan's look.

-Turhan Aswan. He's dead, too.

-Oh.

-And, what about the other guy? I think he's our key man.

-Strange.

-How so?

-His movements were exaggerated and he kept hiding his face. Tommy said he turned into a monster and, then, a woman.

-Tommy's mom said something about that to Nathalie Montaigne.

-That Frenchwoman? She was there that night. I didn't know who she was at the time. I don't think anybody did.

-Did you see anything like what Tommy saw, Teresa?

-I'll just say it. I did see a woman where I thought a man had been standing. But, it was dark and it started to snow. I'm really not sure.

-What did this woman look like?

-Like some wax figure. I could understand Tommy being afraid. She was so thin looking even with an overcoat on. She looked like a corpse standing there.

-Would you recognize her if you saw her again?

-I couldn't forget that face.

Teresa put the proverbial two and two together,

-Did she kill Tommy, Mr. Mendez?

-She's our number one suspect.

-And, that man at the store today? Was that her accomplice because I don't think it was her. I got a good look at him. His movements were normal...for a killer, that is. And, he was definitely a man.

The young girl smiled for the first time.

-I do know the difference.

That was a Saturday: one murder and one close call. And, one death: Erica Mills. Dr. Claire Ingram and Dr. Richard Aster were each performing a second autopsy and every conceivable blood and chemical test they could come up with. So far, they were coming up with virtually nothing: no indication of an unknown disease or venom or poison of any kind.

Lt. Donovan, Sgt. Rayno, and Edward Mendez had run into a stone wall. Their two killers had done a vanishing act. They had no more witnesses – or so they thought. No leads and no tangible suspects – yet.

Part Two
The Hunt

Chapter One
Thursday, September 9, 1948
Dr. Frank Moreland

MARY RILEY offered Edward Mendez a cup of coffee which the P. I. gratefully accepted. It had been a long week and a frustrating one. Should he even be here? Was he wasting his time on something that really didn't matter to anyone but himself? He took a sip of the strong and delicious coffee. How come his coffee never came out this way? And, why hadn't he told Yolanda about his visit to Professor Moreland today?

-Mr Mendez? Professor Moreland will see you now.

He had been so deep in thought that he didn't hear the intercom on Mary Riley's desk.

-Oh! I was a million mies off.

-It's right down the corridor. Good luck.

-Thanks, Miss Riley. I think I'll need it.

Edward got up and walked down the corridor toward Professor Moreland's office. He knocked on the door. Was he starting to perspire? Would the Professor mind if he smoked? He sure hoped not.

Edward knocked on the door.

-Please, come in, Mr. Mendez.

He walked into a well lit office with the rays of the morning sun streaming through the partially opened window. Professor Moreland stood up to greet him.

-Mr. Mendez, pleased to meet you. I've read about you in the papers. Please, sit down.

Edward sat down across from Professor Moreland. He noted the neat and organized desk and the man sitting behind it. The professor was a handsome man of about fifty or fifty-five who looked his age but in a handsome and distinguished way. He had a full head of snow white hair and a full matching moustache. He was slim and about Edward's height. His suit was well-cut and he sat there with his suit jacket open. Edward, himself, felt kind of chilly so he turned up his jacket collar.

-Professor Moreland, good to meet you. Miss Riley has spoken highly of you.

-I'm flattered. And, now, Mr. Mendez, what can I do for you.

This guy didn't waste any time. Edward liked that and returned the favor.

-I'm missing a few critical hours of my life, Professor. I'm hoping that you can point me in the right direction in finding them.

-Do you mean temporary amnesia?

-You could put it like that; but, I think it's a little more complex than your run-of-the-mill amnesia case.

-Why don't you tell me everything from the beginning.

Edward did just that. He didn't spare the Professor any detail and, yet, his story was brief.

-Fascinating, Mr. Mendez. At first, I was very much tempted to refer you to a psychiatrist friend of mine who specializes in amnesia victims. I still might do that. But, the jump in time and space...from your office to an ice skating rink. And, you recall nothing in the interim?

-Not a damned thing Professor. And, would you mind if I lit up.

-Please do. I smoke a pipe myself. I'm glad you broke the ice. Light up!

Edward lit up and took a pretty deep drag on his Lucky. Better. Now, he could really relax.

-Mr. Mendez...I want you to think and smoke as many cigarettes as you'd like. I enjoy the aroma of tobacco. I want you to try and pinpoint the last moment of memory at your office just before you awakened on the ice.

-To be honest, Professor, I'm kind of assuming that I was in my office. I remember riding by subway to get there. And, I don't know why I would do that because I've got my own car. But, I could swear that I was in my office before I blacked out.

Professor Moreland finished lighting his pipe.

-Mr. Mendez, would you have normally visited an ice rink? Had you been dating Miss Estravades prior to the missing time?

-No. I never even heard of the chick. I am an ice hockey fan; but I had no interest in figure skating.

-And, no one saw you physically placed on to the ice?

-No. Yolanda nearly tripped over me.

-So, you found yourself in a location that was, up to that point, unknown to you.

Professor Moreland reached into a desk drawer and took out a type written manuscript.

-My magnum opus. It's based on my theory and research into the space/time continuum.

-Miss Riley mentioned that you were working on it.

-She's proven an invaluable help to my research. Anyway, Mr. Mendez, it's my belief that you just might have "jumped" through time and space. You don't recall those few hours because you never actually lived them.

-You lost me, Professor.

-I'll try to explain. We live from measured moment to measured moment. Think of time set down in a ruler: one that's used by your typical student. You walk along this ruler from one to two to three, etc. But, you, Mr. Mendez, jumped from one to three…skipping number two altogether. You jumped through time and space. The questions are: how and why?

Edward took out another cigarette.

-I can answer one of those questions, Professor Moreland: the why of it. I had a job to do and key people to meet. It's called saving the world.

Edward explained about his exploits in Egypt and Marlena Lake. Professor Moreland was duly impressed.

-Extraordinary. That indeed answers the question of why. Now, as to the "how" of it.

-That, I can't answer.

-I think that you can. When you jumped time and space, were you shifted to another time and place or even another dimension? Were there no flashbacks during your time in Egypt?

-Only one. I saw a group of people sitting around a table.

-What were they doing?

-I think they were holding a seance.

Professor Moreland leaned forward in his chair.

-Did you recognize anyone there? Think, Mr. Mendez, it could be extremely important.

-They looked familiar…like people I might have met once and never thought about again.

-Good answer. Where were they?

-As far as I could make out, the room was lit only by one candle.

-Then, it was a seance that they were conducting.

Professor Moreland sat back and puffed on his pipe.

-Shamus, I'd like to you undergo hypnosis. I can recommend someone if you're willing.

-I'm willing, Professor; but, not at the present time. I'm pretty busy right now and I've got no time for side trips.

-I understand. You know, I'd like to meet this Marlena Lake.

-Your predecessor did — much to his chagrin.

-I read about that. But, she sounds like a fascinating woman.

-That, Professor, you can say again!

Edward got up to leave and, then, sat back down again.

-Professor, I almost forgot. When I went back to my office that next day, I found a set of photographs and news articles about atom bomb tests and the two bombings on Japan.

-And, you've no memory of having placed these photos and news articles in your files?

-You guessed it. But, the writing on the back was in my handwriting.

-Anything odd about these photos?

-Yes. There were these white specks on them that weren't specks. It's like they were coming out of the mushroom cloud.

-Professor Lange was concerned about the affect of these atomic tests on the rotation of the earth. I share those concerns.

-What about those white specks?

-Could be a flaw in the print or debris from the blast itself. I would need to see the photos.

-But, you've got a theory? I can tell, Professor Moreland. My P. I. gut instinct is kicking in.

-You must be good at your job. Yes. I have a theory. The energy expended in an atomic blast is so intense and concentrated, it could just momentarily rip open the fabric of time. Conceivably, it could be used as a means on transfer from one dimension to another or even from one planet to another. I know it sounds fantastic, but so is the atom bomb.

Edward got up to leave. And, this time, he stayed standing.

-Professor, it's been a real pleasure. I've got a lot to think about, And, I can arrange a meeting, if you like, with Miss Marlena Lake.

The Professor also stood up to shake hands with Edward.

-Please do; but at your convenience.

-And, about that hypnosis…maybe. I'll let you know.

-Good day, Mr. Mendez.

-Goodby, Professor.

Professor Moreland watched Edward Mendez leave his office. He liked the young man and was impressed with his intelligence and perception. But, he was puzzled. Had Edward Mendez actually "skipped" time to land in an ice rink in midtown Manhattan? Interesting. Even more interesting if such a thing could be proven. The laws of physics would have to be re-written.

He rang for his secretary, Mary Riley. He wanted to discuss something with her…something that was beginning to worry him more and more with each passing day. She came in with her steno pad ready to take dictation.

-Good. You may need that steno pad, Miss Riley. A running journal should be taken of upcoming events even if my fears prove to be groundless.

-What is it, Professor Moreland? Does it have to do with the weather?

-Yes. But, the weather is the effect and not the cause. The earth, Miss Riley may be drifting off into space.

Mary Riley closed her eyes for a moment. When she opened them, she was her old self: full of questions.

-This is the result of what happened back in December of last year? It must be.

-That seems pretty certain. And, it may not be dire.

-But, you fear that it is.

-I wouldn't say that. The earth may have gone into an extended elliptical orbit throwing the familiar seasons out of whack, if you would.

-But, that would mean that the earth would be nearing the sun, once again, and temperatures should rise.

-Maybe.

-Please, go on. I know you want to say something dreadful, don't you?

-This new elliptical orbit may propel the earth straight out of the solar system or propel it straight into the sun.

Mary Riley once again closed her eyes.

Chapter Two
Friday, September 10, 1948
An Invitation

IT WAS a Friday morning and Edward Mendez, P. I. sat behind his desk looking up at the ceiling. His sister, Nella, was sitting at her usual portable table doing the monthly accounts. The mailman walked in and dropped off the morning mail. He was friendly with Edward and Nella. They were nice people who took the time to talk to him and not just out of politeness.

-Haven't seen Jack around, shamus. He been sick or something?

Edward looked blank for a second. He'd been so busy with his latest investigation that he hadn't noticed.

-I don't know. I guess he must be.

-Not like young Jack not to tell his boss.

-No. It isn't. He likes his job well enough.

-That's what he tells us. Never know what these young boys are thinking.

-He's a kid. Maybe he got ants in his pants and just wanted to take a few days off.

-Maybe.

Nella spoke up.

-Adam, are you sure Jack didn't speak to his boss?

-Positive. Just spoke to Ronnie who put in a call to Jack's mom.

-Did he reach her?

-Miss Nella, that's the strange part. She hasn't heard from the boy in days. She's thinking of calling the cops.

-I hope he's all right.

-We're all kinda' worried. I can tell you that. Might be a case for you, shamus.

Edward lit a cigarette.

-I hope not. But, as soon as I've got some free time, I'll check into it.

The mailman said his goodbyes and left. Brother and sister looked at each other and smiled. The mailman was a gossip, but for Edward that could be useful. Adam knew everyone in the building and everything that went on in the building.

-He'd make a pretty good amateur sleuth, Adam would.

-Edward, still no new leads on the little boy's killer?

-A couple of witnesses, but we're not too close to nailing him.

-The case won't go cold, will it?

-Not if I can help it, sis.

-I was thinking about the murder of that teacher up at Hunter College a few months ago.

-What about it?

-His killer was never caught either.

-Trying to make me feel good?

-It could be the same man who killed little Tommy Burton, couldn't it?

Edward thought about the possibility for a second.

-What makes you ask, sis?

-The night when Henry Vandor tried to kill himself; Turhan Aswan was there and he had an accomplice.

Edward flicked some of the ash from his cigarette into the glass ashtray and continued on his sister's train of thought.

-Tommy was a witness to that little incident. And, Professor Gifford had a fragment of some Sumerian manuscript connected to the dead Mr. Aswan.

-Edward, you can identify Tommy's killer and so can Miss Montaigne, right?

-Keep it going, sis.

-Did you get a good look at Professor's Gifford's killer?

He shrugged.

-No. He barreled right past me and took off like a bat out of hell.

Nella was a little disappointed.

-Oh, that's too bad.

Edward took his feet off the desk.

-Hold on. Just hold on! Henriette Miller. She was a student in that class. And, if I'm not mistaken, not too much gets by her. And, if I'm not mistaken, again, she gave a description at police HQ on the night of the murder.

-Did the police create a sketch of the man?

-I'll check on it. But, if they haven't, I know someone who's an artist...sort of.

Nella smiled.

-Of course. Yolanda. She did a sketch of Victoria and me.

-Let me put in a call to Sgt. Rayno. He'll know who to get in touch with And, Nella, thanks for the tip.

A sketch had been made of the suspect who killed Professor Daniel Gifford back in January of that same year. Yes. Edward wanted to see it; but, not just yet. He wanted to speak to Henriette Miller first and he was gonna' bring Yolanda in on this.

Edward hung up the phone with Sgt. Rayno and was about to dial Henriette Miller's number when he spotted an over-sized envelope on his desk. It was square, white and embossed: an invitation with a return address. He opened it up. It was an invitation to a séance to be held next Friday at 11:00 A.M. at 30 Park Ave.

-A morning séance?

-Edward? What did you say? And, what are you smiling about?

-It seems I've been invited to a séance, Nella.

-When?

-Next Friday morning in mid-town in a swanky Park Ave. apartment.

-That's an unusual time of day for a séance, isn't it? I believe there's a solar eclipse occurring just about then.

Edward nodded. He read about the eclipse in the paper. It was a pretty big event for New York City. He looked over at Nella.

-Wanna' come? Might be a lot of fun.

-As a matter of fact, I would. Do you think that Yolanda would mind?

-Not a bit, I'm sure. She likes you a lot.

-And, I like her. By the way, Edward, who's the invitation from?

-Marlena Lake.

Edward Mendez, P. I. had a date with Henriette Miller, college student, that night. It was Lt. Donovan who had the actual date with the girl. Edward had his own date, Yolanda. It was that same Friday evening and the two couples gathered in Yolanda's apartment for a night cap. The double date was carefully and deliberately planned to look just like that: casual and off-handed and above suspicion. Edward wasn't taking any chances with this witness.

Lt. Donovan and Yolanda were in the kitchen mixing drinks and putting the finishing touches on some canapés that Yolanda had prepared. The two of them were actually getting along for a change, Edward thought.

-Yolanda? Congratulations on your bronze medal win.

-Thank you. I'm still going to try for the gold next year.

-Good for you. So, what do you think of your boyfriend's latest case?

-For some reason, it's frightening. Young people dying of old age. Could it be the beginning of some epidemic?

-Let's hope not. I don't think it is; but, it is bizarre, all right.

The Lieutenant laughed out loud.

-Oh, what's so funny?

-I'm laughing at the trend of my own thoughts. Each and every time I come across something out of the ordinary or downright bizarre, one name pops into this thick Irish skull.

-Not Edward's name.

-No. But, you do know her. Marlena Lake.

Now, it was Yolanda's turn to laugh.

-I should have guessed. The bizarre is her specialty and how she comes by her information, who knows.

-That's exactly what I'd like to know.

-She's a character. We don't exactly get along. I don't think she likes her own sex very much. But, since her son's death, she and her daughter, Susan, have gotten much closer.

-I noticed that back in December of last year. Susan seems like an intelligent girl. I don't sense any malice in her.

-She's very sensible and one of the few people who actually challenges her mother.

-Good for her. So, she wouldn't be a party to anything criminal, then?

-Not Susan.

-Good. I'm real glad to hear that.

Yolanda didn't like the way Lt. Donovan said that.

Edward and Henriette were on the sofa sharing an awkward moment. He liked the girl, but there was something almost military about her. The way she held herself so erect and her straight-to-the point answers as if she were in a witness box. You either liked this girl or you couldn't stand her; there was no middle ground.

-Henriette?

The young girl smiled warmly at the detective.

-Yes, Mr. Mendez? You would like to ask me something?

-Call me Edward.

-Edward. Of course, William has told me what you need me to do. And, I have thought about it all day. I am ready to help you.

This girl was efficient and straight to the point, but pleasant enough.

-Good girl. Do you remember what that killer looked like: the one who bumped off Professor Gifford?

-Yes. I have an eye for detail. He was taller than William who I believe is six feet tall. The killer was at least six foot two inches and wiry in body frame and movement. He wore a Fedora hat very much like yours, Edward.

Henriette took a deep breath and continued.

-And, now of course, his face. It resembled a mask: a white, paste-like mask. There is a name for it; but, I can't recall what it is. It rendered his face featureless with dark, coal-like eyes. If he had remained motionless, one could have easily mistaken him for a window display mannequin.

Edward was about to light a cigarette, but stopped.

-My God.

-Have I helped you at all, Edward?

-I'll say.

Lt. Donovan and Yolanda walked in, each carrying a tray of drinks and canapés.

-Well, Mendez, has Henriette helped us? And, you're about to burn yourself with that match.

Edward dropped the match into the ashtray.

-Miss Henriette has helped, all right. Tommy Burton and Professor Daniel Gifford were killed by the same man. But-

Lt. Donovan and Yolanda sat down and started handing out drinks.

-But?

-We've got a second killer on our hands.

Lt. Donovan laughed; but, he didn't really feel like laughing.

-I think I've lived through something like this not too long ago. Sorry, Mendez, I interrupted.

-Like I said, we've got two killers on our hands: the one who tried bumping off Teresa Farmer last Saturday and our old friend from the train station.

Lt. Donovan lit a cigarette, inhaled and slowly exhaled.

-Okay. We gotta' lure at least one of these bastards out into the open.

-Agreed. But, how do we go about it – as if I didn't know. And, thanks for the drink, baby.

Yolanda smiled and volunteered a solution.

-Lure him out with bait. Like a piece of cheese for a mouse.

Lt. Donovan nodded.

-No. A rat…a dirty, filthy rat who goes around killing little boys. And, a pretty girl by the name of Debbie Stone should do the trick for this rat.

Henriette spoke up.

-But, that would place the girl in terrible danger.

-We'll be there: me and Mendez, here, and half the precinct.

Henriette wasn't convinced.

-These men must be very clever. To kill people in broad daylight is quite daring and brazen. Please, William, don't underestimate them. And, I don't have a good feeling about this.

-To be honest, Henriette, neither do I. But, we've gotta' do something.

Yolanda took a drag on Edward's cigarette.

-Edward?

-What is it, baby?

-What about that couple out in Long Island?

-The Sandersons?

-Yes. Which killer executed them?

-Take your pick. I don't know. But, I'm betting it's one or the other of the two we're after.

He was just about finishing his scotch and soda when a thought popped into his head.

-Hey, Lieutenant, how about if both killers show up and they bring some company with them?

-We'll handle it. We've done this sort of thing before. And, besides, Mendez, you'll be there to help out. How can we lose?

Chapter Three

KENNETH NG was driving down Fifth Ave. with Miss Linda Kawano in the passenger seat beside him. Both driver and passenger were deep in thought as the sleek, black car maneuvered through the evening traffic of the city.

Mr. Kenneth Ng had been in this country a good many years. He came to America with his mother and father in the year 1899 only days before the turn of the century. Mr. Ng was a teenager of seventeen. He and his family were "moved" to the Chinatown section of the city to live in abject poverty. His father was a tradesman who sold whatever he could get his hands on in a make-shift storefront along Canal St. The inventory consisted of used and incomplete encyclopedias, used books sans covers, and odds and ends that Mr. Ng could collect from the more affluent sections of the city. The family lived in the small back room with the family cat who fended off the vermin that Mrs. Ng was so terrified of.

Kenneth Ng wanted to go to university with the hope of going to medical school. But, as the months evolved into years, he saw how his dreams clashed with the grim reality that surrounded his life.

It was 1901 and he was nineteen when he met Mr. Josef Antonio near the excavation site of the soon to be completed New York City subway system. Kenneth Ng was staring into the deep trench of a subway tunnel that was now being covered over. He looked forward to riding it uptown on the east side of the city where the wealthy lived. He was contemplating a life of crime…perhaps, as the first Asian cat burglar in Manhattan. The prospect amused him as much as embittered him.

Mr. Josef Antonio approached the teenager.

-Good evening.

-Good evening.

-I'll introduce myself: Mr. Josef Antonio.

For the first time in his nineteen years, Kenneth Ng stammered.

-My name is Kenneth Ng.

-Looking into the future of a near completed transit system? Or are you looking into your own personal future?

Kenneth Ng smiled.

-Both.

-Are your prospects well aspected?

-No. But, I will change that.

-Your English is quite good.

-Why shouldn't it be?

-Do not be defensive with me, young man. Accept a compliment with due graciousness.

-I apologize for my bad manners. I was raised better than that.

-Apology accepted. Let us go into that tea shop.

-I have no money.

-I do. I have much money. And, one day sooner than you expect, you will have the equivalent of my wealth without resorting to a life of crime.

-How did you-

-How did I ascertain your thoughts? I looked into your eyes, Mr. Ng and saw the rawness of your soul. Come. I am thirsty and so are you. We'll speak about wealth, immortality, and a different line of crime from the one you were contemplating.

Kenneth Ng claimed his first victim later that evening. The immortality that Mr. Antonio promised had been fulfilled and the wealth from their selected victims lifted Kenneth Ng and his family from poverty.

Miss Linda Kawano was the daughter of rich merchants who dealt in rare and exotic gems that more often than not were for "sale" on the black market to the highest bidder. These gems were obtained through methods of blackmail and out right assassins. Miss Kawano was no stranger to crime which is why she was not a victim of Mr. Kenneth Ng, but a sort out member for Mr. Antoni's developing cult. Like Kenneth Ng, she also was approached by Mr. Antonio to join and reap the benefits and hazards of immortality. She didn't need much persuading. Her mother was long deceased and her father was growing old and crippled with arthritis. His black market days were coming to an end and his ambitious daughter did not want to live on an inherited and limited income.

Mr. Antonio was pleased with his two new members. Immortality could be a lonely burden.

Rick Wasserman had just proposed marriage to Jennifer Caswell on the beach in the Hamptons. It was a romantic but sloppy proposal: suntan lotion and champagne had splashed on to the newspaper and the engagement ring kept sliding off Jennifer's finger.

-Don't worry. It's 14 karat gold. You can have it sized down.

-I love it. A blue sapphire and diamonds…my favorite gem stones.

A figure walking along the beach caught Rick's eye.

-We've got company.

Which was unusual for this time of year: it was early October and the Hamptons were pretty much deserted until spring.

The figure approached the young couple. It was Josef Antonio who wasted no time in his own proposal.

-Mr. Rick Wasserman? Miss Jennifer Caswell? My name is Josef Antonio and I have an unusual proposition to set before you. Do not interrupt me, Mr. Wasserman. If you and your fiancé refuse my proposal you will never encounter me again.

He addressed Rick Wasserman.

-Mr. Wasserman, you are in financial debt. You are on the point of bankruptcy with creditors making your life quite miserable. You are not about to marry into money. You will pardon my frankness, Miss Caswell. Your family name goes back several generations; but, the bulk of your wealth is gone: a failure to move with the times. I can change all that; and, you both will have to change in the process.

Mr. Antonio passed for a moment to let his words sink in. The couple was taken aback, but could offer no protest. All that Josef Antonio stated was true.

-Good. You recognize the futility of protest. And, now, I will tell you of my proposal.

The year was 1923.

Freda and Hans Becker would be branded traitors to their country as soon as the United States entered into World War II. At the present time, they were Nazi sympathizers and had helped relay military information through their "delicatessen:" a business that barely eked a profit. The brother and sister knew that they were being watched and that it was only a matter of time before they were arrested. They didn't dare try to leave the country. All they could do was wait and pray that their services would no longer be needed. But, Hans Becker knew better. They would always be on "call" as sleepers: never knowing when you would be called upon to do whatever dirty work you were ordered to do. Always looking over your shoulder and jumping out of your skin every time the telephone rang. Had it been worth it? No. The compensation barely kept them afloat in their lower east side apartment that wasn't much better than a slum. And, worry had taken its toll on the two of them. They looked ten years older than they should have with Freda Becker turning to drugs to quiet her nerves. Her brother hit the bottle and wasn't too choosey about what brand of liquor he drank.

When Josef Antonio walked into their store, these two miscreants were easy pickings for him. Why did he recruit them? They were devious, resourceful in their own way, and desperate. Lars Becker was a sociopath and would never fit into society as an everyday citizen. Freda Becker was an angry individual: angry at life in general and at her reflection in the mirror each morning in particular. By any standard this woman was ugly and her temperament didn't help matters...maybe the promise of money would?

Josef Antonio had his cult assembled and they were loyal: money and immortality had purchased their allegiance. Eventually, he could send them out to obtain brain stem fluid and even recruit outside members who could move about much more freely than any of the cult members themselves could. Or had he overestimated his members' "recruiting" abilities? Some things a leader should really do for himself.

Chapter Four

Sunday, September 12, 1948
Bowery Mishap

OFFICER PATRICK Mitchell had been with the New York City Police Force for fifteen years. He spent his first three years as a patrol officer "pounding" a beat down by the Bowery and then, Chinatown. He loved his work and had made more arrests than any other cop in his district. He stood at an even six feet and had the physique of an Atlas. He also had a right hook that could knock the sense out of any opponent. Officer Mitchell had the looks of a Hollywood movie star: dark, curly hair, blue eyes, a strong jaw and straight features. He'd been married once, but his wife had deserted him for his lack of ambition. She wanted him to rise in the ranks of the police force; but, he was content with being a patrol cop and mingling with the public face-to-face. It's what he loved to do; not sitting behind some desk.

Officer Mitchell was in his patrol car now and riding down Broadway toward the Bowery section of the city. His partner, Officer Roscoe Jackson, was sitting next to him and smoking a cigarette. Both men were relaxed but alert. They knew their job and were always ready for action of any sort. And, tonight, the two cops were going to encounter plenty of action.

-Tonight, we can prove ourselves to Mr. Antonio. We go to one of those flop houses on the lower east side and help ourselves to a victim or two. Should be easy. I foresee no problem. Do you?

Hans Becker asked that question of the three people in the car in his arrogant and guttural manner. Not everyone in the group liked this uncouth man. Jennifer Caswell most of all detested this cretin. She answered him.

-Does Mr. Antonio know we're out and about, Mr. Becker? He usually does this himself or takes one of us with him. He does know what we're up to, doesn't he?

Mr. Becker spit out his answer. He didn't like Miss Caswell and was aware of her opinion of him.

-We have all gone with Mr. Antonio. He'll be pleased. You must trust me.

And, that was just it. Aside from his sister, Freda Becker, no one in that car did trust him. Miss Caswell continued to question their driver.

-Why aren't Mr. Ng and Miss Kawano here with us? You didn't tell them about this little foray, did you, Mr. Becker?

-I give an account to Mr. Antonio and no one else. Mr. Ng and Miss Kawano are mere members like ourselves.

Mr. Wasserman, who was sitting behind Mr. Becker, disagreed.

-Mr. Ng and Miss Kawano have gone out by themselves. They've hunted down victims. We haven't. It's not too late to turn back.

Freda Becker looked back at Mr. Wasserman.

-We must learn to acquire their hunting skills. We cannot remain dependent on the others. I don't like that dependence and neither should you. Where is your backbone, Mr. Wasserman?

-Just watch what you say to me, lady.

Miss Caswell jumped in.

-Are we almost there? If we're going to "prove" ourselves, let's just do it. All this talk and arguing isn't doing anyone any good.

Hans Becker smiled at his perceived triumph.

-Miss Caswell, you are quite correct. I've visited this spot. It's out of the way and only the so-called down and out frequent there. These people are despondent and defeated by life. They won't offer anything but token resistance.

Mr. Wasserman disagreed.

-You hope. When someone's fighting for his life, you might be surprised at the fight he'll put up. Don't be too damned sure of yourself, Becker.

-You bore me, Mr. Wasserman. You're arrogant, even for a Jew.

-You Nazi pig! Just stop this car and step the fuck out. I'll show you how bored I am.

Miss Becker now stepped in.

-Enough! The two of you will be enough to defeat this effort tonight.

Miss Caswell agreed.

-Rick, she's right. Ignore him and just focus on what has to be done. You can argue about it later when we get back to the hotel. Do we have the equipment that we'll need?

Rick Wasserman was still fuming.

-We've got it. It's in the medical bag right at my feet.

Miss Caswell put a comforting hand on his broad shoulder.

-Good. Now, I suggest that we all save our strength. We're going to need it.

Mr. Becker was still smiling.

It was just past dusk at the Bowery station. The station wasn't exactly a flop house; the three upper floors were cheap, one bedrooms that could be rented for the night or for an extended stay of a month...the monthly renters were in the minority. On the main floor one could come in from the street and watch the new television set. There was a couch and a couple of dilapidated armchairs with inner springs just about ready to pop out of them.

Two men and a women were enjoying the television program and momentarily forgetting about their lives of desperation. The two men were alcoholics and the woman was a dope addict. All three had lost their jobs and apartments. They wandered the streets of the city and usually ended up where they were at the present time. The clothes on their backs had been given to them by the Salvation Army. All three had chosen not to stay at that holding place because it would mean attending services and doing "voluntary" work. The two men were not religious and any form of work to them was an anathema; although the woman, who had been a practical nurse, had considered staying.

One of the men, Vince Edelman, had been an attorney. His practice had not prospered and he had no back-up: no living relatives and no friends who could assist him financially He was forced to leave his apartment and sleep in the subway. His confidence was broken along with his spirit.

The other man was a born drifter. He'd given up on society and had made his peace with his out-of-bounds life. What was the use in struggling? Everyone ended up in the grave sooner or later.

Adele Jones was thinking about the possibility of religion now. Why not turn to religion? It couldn't hurt, could it? What on earth did she have to lose? Nothing. She had nothing so what was there to lose in the gamble? She was warming up to the idea.

Officers Mitchell and Jackson were rounding the corner of Broadway and heading due east along Canal St. Their eyes were adjusting to the oncoming darkness and both men were alert and ready for action. They didn't have much to say to each other because they understood and respected each other. They'd been partners for the past thirteen months. Officer Jackson was one of the few black cops on the police force and he was eager to learn all he could through first-hand street experience. Both officer were good with their fists and were crack shots. Not too many criminals got past them. Their reputations in their precinct ranked high.

-Hey, Pat, look over there.

-Yeah. Kind of an unlikely group to be walking about here.

-Could be they're slumming. Rich folk like to do that sort of thing.

-Makes 'em feel superior handing out dimes, but...

-I know. They look like they know where they're heading. Look at the tall guy. What's he carrying with him?

Officer Mitchell could just about make it out.

-If I didn't know any better, I'd say it was a medical bag. You know, the kind that doctors use.

-You think that dude's some kind of doctor?

-No, Roscoe, I don't. Let's tail 'em. Something tells me they're up to no good.

Officer Mitchell slowed the patrol car down and kept a twenty yard distance between it and the four suspects. It wasn't long before they entered a local hostel and resting area; both patrolmen were familiar with it.

-Hey, Pat. park this car, man.

-You bet.

Officer Mitchell had to double-park the squad car. They got out and headed into the hostel...known as one of the better flop houses.

Jennifer Caswell and Rick Wasserman entered the lobby and their presence caused an immediate stir among the three guests: at first, resentment and then uneasiness. The three guests tried not to stare at the new arrivals, but they couldn't help themselves. Miss Caswell was too pretty and Mr. Wasserman was imposing in his height and build.

Miss Caswell approached Adele and introduced herself. She would be the first victim.

-May I sit next to you?

-Sure, honey.

Miss Caswell sat down and withdrew a perfume atomizer from her handbag.

-Would you mind? Some people don't like perfume. You're not allergic, are you?

-Never had any to be allergic to. But, you go ahead and spray yourself.

Miss Caswell pointed the atomizer at Adele and sprayed it full force into the woman's face. The woman gagged and fell off the couch on to the floor. The two men saw what happened and rushed over to help, but Mr. Wasserman stood in their way. Miss Becker and Mister Becker burst into the lobby brandishing guns. The two homeless men stopped dead in their tracks. They were no fools.

Mister Becker spoke to the two men.

-Go back to where you were sitting. Make no attempt to leave or call for help. We will kill you if you try. Tell me that you understand.

-We got ya', pal. Just take it easy with those guns, okay?

-Keep quiet.

Mr. Wasserman put the medical bag on the floor and was about ready to open it when the door burst open and two tough looking cops came in.

Officer Mitchel was the first to speak out.

-What the hell's goin' on here?

-Put that gun down, lady. You, too, pal. Now! Or we'll blow it out of your fuckin' hand.

Mr. and Miss Becker complied. Cowards don't usually argue with authority.

Mr. Wasserman straightened up while holding on to the medical bag that was still open. He didn't have a chance to latch it closed.

-What's in the bag, pal?

That was Officer Mitchell.

-None of your damned business. We haven't done anything wrong.

Both Officers laughed at that one. Officer Roscoe pointed his gun at Mr. Wasserman.

-Just put it back on the floor. Hey, Pat, I think that woman on the floor needs help. What'd you do to her, lady?

Officer Roscoe knelt by Adele and felt her pulse.

-She's dead. Looks like she choked on something real bad. What's that you're holding?

Miss Caswell smiled prettily and didn't answer.

-Okay, we're all gonna' take a trip down to HQ. Hey, Roscoe, there's a phone over there; but, let's cuff these bastards.

Miss Caswell got up, holding on to her atomizer...getting ready to use it. But, Officer Patrick Mitchell was not to be taken in by this amateur. He saw the atomizer as a weapon and knocked it out of Miss Caswell's hand. Mr. Wasserman made a grab of the medical bag, but again, Officer Mitchell, was ready for this. He belted Mr. Wasserman on the side of the head sending the big man sprawling on to the threadbare rug.

Officer Jackson went to cuff Mr. Becker. He saw that his partner didn't need any help with those two. He cuffed Mr. Becker and went to do the same to Becker's sister; she tripped him and Officer Jackson landed on his knees giving Miss Becker time to scoop up the gun she had been ordered to drop. She got a hold of it and aimed it at Officer Jackson who saw this and made a grab for her legs. He got her off balance before she could aim properly. She fell with her back to the floor and cried out in pain.

However, in taking care of Miss Becker, Officer Jackson was forced to turn his back on Mr. Becker who flung himself, handcuffs and all, on to Officer Jackson. He stunned the cop. Officer Mitchell came over but Miss Becker had enough time to recover. She had her gun and fired point blank at the ex-boxer. He took the shot in the upper abdomen and fell to the floor but still conscious.

Miss Caswell ran over to Mr. Wasserman, helped him up, and grabbed the medical bag on the floor.

-Let's get out of here. Everybody, hurry!

It wouldn't be so easy. Officer Jackson, now recovered, made a flying "scissors" leap and caught Mr. Becker on the calves who fell head long into his fleeing sister. Miss Caswell came to her partner's-in-crime rescue. She sprayed Officer Jackson in the face with her atomizer, blinding him and leaving him gasping for air.

Officer Mitchell who was bleeding profusely took aim at Mr. Wasserman and shot him in the thigh. The criminal cried out in pain, but kept running for the door. Officer Mitchell was't quite finished. He didn't discriminate when it came to taking down criminals: women were as much fair game as men. He took real careful aim and shot Miss Becker in the left shoulder. She, like her comrade cried out in pain.

Officer Mitchell got to his feet and was ready to fire again when Mr. Wasserman turned unexpectedly and knifed him The knife went straight into Officer Patrick Mitchell's heart. He fell to the floor...dead.

The criminals made their escape.

-You bungling idiots. Who was the one who stabbed the police officer? Who was it among you fools?

Mr. Wasserman confessed that it was he.

Mr. Josef Antonio was beside himself with rage. How could they ever have had the audacity to undertake such an operation by themselves? It took years...no, decades...of practice and cunning to go out on the kill. And, these fools thought to do it themselves. He should have known better than to have taken a Jew into the group. Arrogant. They were all cut from the same rotten cloth. But, he couldn't place the blame entirely on Wasserman. No. All four of them had freely taken part and now a respected and even beloved police officer had been knifed and killed. His fellow cops would surely be seeking revenge in the name of justice. And, Mr. Antonio couldn't blame them.

And, there had been another officer there besides…and he survived to lead the police vigilante squad. Not to mention the other two hapless would-be victims — all of whom had escaped unharmed and could identify the four cult members.

More than ever, the group had to go underground. Mr. Antonio knew that he needed someone with skill and resourcefulness to operate as a conduit for the group.

Antonio paced about in the hotel room. His gaze rested upon one member and then another. And, to go out on the hunt just after dusk? Imbeciles! The early hours of the morning were the time to go on the kill; it was those hours when most of the city was asleep and vulnerable.

He sat down on a chair. At least Mr. Kenneth Ng and Miss Linda Kawano had better sense. He could trust them to an extent. Still…someone had to be found to lure victims for the needed brain stem fluid.

Miss Kawano spoke.

-Mr. Antonio, I know what you are thinking.

-Then, tell me.

-Mr. Edward Mendez might do quite nicely. Mr. Ng has been to his office and I think that we should look into the matter.

-Yes, Miss Kawano. I quite agree. Thank you.

Chapter Five
Monday, September 13, 1948
Abduction

IT WAS a Monday afternoon and the second week of classes at St. Michael's H.S. The students were being let out and the all-girl student body couldn't be happier. Among those students in the Highland Park section of Brooklyn was Debbie Stone. She was one of the prettiest and most popular girls in her Junior class. And, if she played her cards right, she just might be voted Prom Queen.

The sidewalk was crowded with girls walking in small groups of two's and three's. Debbie was talking with one of her girlfriends about the surprise French quiz that their teacher had sprung on them. Neither girl was too delighted; but, they decided to laugh it off and maybe even study a little harder...maybe.

The streets were crowded with parked cars and the park opposite the school had more than the usual number of people enjoying the flora and fauna. Edward Mendez, Sgt. Tom Rayno, and Lt. William Donovan were among those "strolling" in the park. They let rumor fly that they were close to apprehending Tommy Burton's murderer with the help of a young, key witness. Hopefully, the bait had been taken.

Debbie Stone had been guarded for days, but this was her first day back at school. Her mother had kept her home the previous week. Reluctantly, Mrs. Stone allowed her daughter to attend classes this week. She was, however, waiting for Debbie at the train station along with a plain clothes police woman.

Two concealed squad cars were parked down the street from the school's entrance. Edward Mendez was lighting a cigarette and getting ready to open the door to his Ford. Sgt. Rayno and Lt. Donovan were in civilian clothes on opposite street corners pretending to look for their "daughters" in the crowd of students.

Cars were driving by on the two way street that separated the park from the high school. There wasn't much traffic, but just enough where one had to be careful of crossing between parked cars.

Debbie and her girlfriend decided to head for the corner and play it safe. The two girls were passing by a gray colored car when a school textbook fell out of the back window.

-Could you just hand that to me, please?

-Sure.

Debbie stooped down to pick up the book when two powerful arms reached out and grabbed her by the shoulders. She was pulled into the car. Debbie's girlfriend screamed and tried to help her friend. Her scream brought Edward racing across the street and nearly getting run over. A shot rang out and Debbie's girlfriend fell dead to the pavement. Most of the girls nearby dropped to the pavement or ran for cover.

The gray car pulled out of its space and, again, Edward was nearly run over. He ran back to his Ford waving his arms to signal the squad car up ahead to block traffic. Edward reached his car and recklessly pulled out of his parking space. Sgt. Rayno and Lt. Donovan got into their respective cars. Lt. Donovan's car was the one to block that particular flow of traffic. He pulled out and almost had that lane of traffic blocked when Debbie's abductors barreled through, side swiping the Lieutenant's left bumper. It didn't stop the criminals, but it "stunned" their vehicle just enough to give Edward a chance to catch up to them. The P. I. was now in pursuit. Lt. Donovan righted his car and followed with Sgt. Rayno right behind him.

The plain clothes men on the street ran over to Debbie's girlfriend, but it was too late. She'd been shot straight through the head. Another "execution" style killing.

Edward saw the criminals' car just ahead of him: a gray '47 Pontiac. He could just make out the man sitting in the back seat. He was tying up Debbie's hands, but the girl was putting up a struggle. The man turned back to look at the P. I. Edward recognized him as the assailant at Grand Central Station. Why hadn't he killed the girl...because he had to know what she knew.

The criminal's car was picking up speed: 40 mph., 50 mph, 60 mph and going faster.

-Man's a fucking maniac. He's gonna' get us all killed.

Edward glanced in his rear view mirror. Lt. Donovan was still behind him. He had to assume that Sgt. Rayno was right behind Lt. Donovan. The four cars pulled on to the Grand Central Expressway. It was just past 3 P. M. so rush hour traffic hadn't kicked in yet.

-The maniac's doing better than 70 mph now. Where the hell in Manhattan is he headed for? He's gonna' try and lose me. Keep your eyes on him, Mendez.

The criminal's car was now weaving in and out of traffic, passing cars and nearly side swiping some of them. They were almost in Manhattan – all four cars dogging each other. Grand Central Station was just up ahead. The criminals' car made a sharp right on to 42nd St., headed crosstown to 5th Ave. turned left and raced downtown. Edward was right behind him.

-Where's Rayno? There he is! A couple of cars behind.

They were now past 39th St. running traffic lights and causing minor accidents along the way. Without warning, the criminals' car veered crosstown. They were headed back uptown and still running every red and amber light until they reached 42nd St. and Park Ave. when the gray car lost control, ran on to the sidewalk and smashed into a lamp post.

The driver got out and made a run for it. The two occupants in the back seat remained inside for a moment. Edward pulled up to the car as the back door opened. The kidnapper came out pulling Debbie with him. The young girl was in tears, but alive and unharmed. The kidnapper held on to his victim and made no attempt to flee. Edward got out of his car and approached them with his gun drawn.

-It's over, pal. Let the girl go.

The kidnapper spoke. Was that a mask he was wearing?

-No, Mr. Mendez. I am going to take this girl with me into that estimable terminal behind us. I will release her when I have disappeared into the crowd of commuters. You will stay where you are.

-That's not gonna' happen. Let her go.

Lt. Donovan's car pulled up and Sgt. Rayno's was right behind him.

The kidnapper continued to address Edward.

-I will not be captured. I have lived far too long to have it end like this.

-You're right about that: you've lived too friggin' long. Now, let-her-go!

-My knife's blade, Mr. Mendez, is pressed into this young girl's back. I will have no compunction in pushing it through to her heart. Now, drop your weapon.

Edward was not about to let this killer get away. He had to stall for time.

-We've got company, pal. You're outnumbered.

If Edward could just distract him enough to look away, he'd have a clear shot at him.

-How do you know my name? Why not tell me yours?

-I have many names. I prefer Josef Antonio.

-Tell me some of your other names.

Edward was starting to perspire.

-Come on, you bastard! Just turn your eyes to the right. It's how I fake out my boxing opponent.

And, the kidnapper did just that.

The P. I. took aim and fired. He hit the kidnapper in the solar plexus. He released the girl and collapsed to the pavement.

Edward rushed over to Debbie who was close to hysterics.

-Debbie, are you hurt?

-I don't think so. Is he dead?

-He's dead, all right.

Lt. Donovan ran over and was joined by Sgt. Rayno.

-Debbie? Go with Sgt. Rayno here. He'll take good care of you.

Lt. Donovan stood in the way.

-Just one thing, Debbie. Did you get a good look at the driver?

-No. I was held down by that terrible man. The two of them didn't say anything- except something about a fun house. I couldn't make it out. It didn't make any sense.

Lt. Donovan turned to Sgt. Rayno.

-Take her up to the precinct, Sgt. And, try to get word to Mrs. Stone that her daughter is safe.

-I'll get her some coffee. And, we'll have a talk if she's up to it.

Lt. Donovan addressed Edward.

-The medics are on their way. I radioed in from my car.

The two men looked at the dead kidnapper.

-He's dead, huh? Too bad.

-I know. He might've fessed up with his last stinking breath.

-What are you looking at, Mendez? He didn't move, did he?

-No.

-But?

Edward squatted down and ran his finger along the dead man's jawline.

-Hey, Donovan, he's wearing some kind of a mask.

-Take it off. Let's see what we've got underneath.

The P. I. peeled off the flesh toned latex mask. He and Lt. Donovan did a double-take. What they saw was a scarred and burnt face of a man.

-Mendez, check his trench coat lining. I've got a hunch.

Edward opened up the dead man's trench coat and unzipped the lining. Another mask fell out and a woman's wig came with it. It all clicked into place. Edward got to his feet holding on to the wig.

-This is what little Tommy saw at the train station that night and it cost him his life.

Lt. Donovan took the wig from Edward.

-It looks like it was attached to the mask. Here. You can see the adhesive.

Edward nodded.

-Pretty clever.

-Clever, all right. But, who the hell was he? Mendez, you got any idea?

-He called himself Josef Antonio. Doesn't that ring a bell, Lieutenant?

-Aswan! He mentioned that name just before he died. He's the guy who supposedly gave the secret of eternal youth to that undertaker. They can keep that rotten secret!

-He might be the one who bumped off Professor Gifford.

-Makes sense.

Edward took a look around them.

-Uh-oh. We got some curious onlookers.

-I'll take care of them. I hear the ambulance siren.

Edward stood there lost in thought for a couple of minutes. Why did this Josef Antonio kill for the sake of a disguise? And, why the hell was he so desperate to kidnap Debbie Stone? The man must have been down-right paranoid – desperate to hold on to his perverted life at any cost – kill whoever he thought he had to kill. And, it bothered Edward that this bastard's accomplice had escaped. His P. I. gut told him that this accomplice was the one who gunned down Patty Kilmeade and probably the Sandersons. And, what about the Mills couple and Missy Wingate? What was the connection?

The P. I. laughed out loud at a stray thought: an invitation to a Friday morning séance...an invitation from none other than Marlena Lake.

-I wonder if she knows anything about any of this? A man wants to keep his disguise...his alter ego a secret at any cost. A hitman murders because someone might have been told something. What had the Sandersons known? What had Patty Kilmeade known? Probably nothing.

The ambulance arrived and took the body away. Lt. Donovan headed uptown. Edward drove crosstown to pick up Yolanda at the ice rink. He lit himself a cigarette.

-A fun house. Debbie mentioned a fun house and so did Erica Mills. Patty Kilmeade said something about Missy Wingate taking walks along the Coney Island boardwalk. Wouldn't that take her past a fun house?

Edward eased his car into the crosstown traffic.

-I wonder if the amusement park is still open?

Victoria Mendez was shopping on the main floor of Macy's Department Store and not finding anything that she cared to purchase. Even the latest perfume had failed to lure the beautiful woman into opening up her wallet. She wasn't in the mood to go to the fashion department and try on clothes. Not today, but maybe there was something in cosmetics that would justify her journey into the city. She headed in that direction.

The main floor wasn't too crowded and there was just enough "hubbub" to keep that lone shopper from feeling too lonely. Victoria stood at the cosmetics counter and was on the point of choosing a new compact. Her old one really had seen better days. She was about to choose a round, gold-toned compact when a woman stopped by the same counter a few feet away from her.

Victoria Mendez glanced at this woman and could see that she wasn't looking at any of the cosmetics. No. She was nervously glancing to her left and right. Her glance fell on Victoria and she quickly turned away. Victoria could see that she was the nervous type. Her blonde hair was pinned up, but strands of hair were sticking all out. The woman's lipstick needed re-touching and, yes, her nose was shiny. And, then, Victoria noticed the hat box that the woman had on her. It was quite lovely: a pale pink with rosettes on the top part of the round hat box. Victoria also noticed how tightly she was holding on to it.

The woman moved closer and spoke to Edward's sister.

-Please, may I ask a favor?

-Of course. But, I don't see how I can help you.

-If you could just walk with me to the exit, that's all.

-I was about to purchase this cosmetics compact.

-Oh, don't let me stop you. Please. Just keep me company until we get to the exit. They won't expect me to be with anybody.

-I beg your pardon?

-Please, make your purchase. I don't think I've been spotted; but, that could change at any moment. Please, hurry.

Victoria purchased her compact and walked with the blonde woman to one of the rear exit doors that let out on to Seventh Avenue. Like her brother, Edward Mendez, she had a sense of adventure and this was a very interesting situation.

When the two women reached the exit.

-Thank you. And, for your own sake, please forget that you ever saw me.

She left Victoria standing on the sidewalk just outside of the world's largest department store.

Victoria boarded the F train to take her home to Brooklyn Heights. The train wasn't crowded and she found herself a seat next to the window. She was about to take out her lipstick and do a bit of a touch up when a man sat down next to her.

-I beg your pardon? Do you mind if I sit here?

-Of course not.

-Thank you. I believe we just came from the same department store: Macy's. I'm always a bit overwhelmed when I go there. It's so big!

-Yes. It is. It's a famous store.

The man sitting next to her was handsome. His hair was turning grey at the temples but his complexion was clear and with a touch of suntan to it. He wore a three piece suit and gray gloves to match the suit.

-I couldn't help but notice that you might have left something behind.

Victoria was puzzled.

-No. I don't think so. I have my handbag and my one purchase.

-But, the hatbox…I don't see it on you now.

-I didn't have any hatbox- Oh! The woman I was speaking to. Yes. She had a very pretty hatbox with her, but it wasn't from Macy's.

The man was silent for a moment.

-Yes. That must be it. I'm sorry to have troubled you. Excuse me.

As abruptly as he sat down, he got up and left the train at the next stop. And, Victoria had to ask herself.

-What in the world was that all about?

Chapter Six

Wednesday, September 15, 1948
Coney Island Fun House

IT WAS Wednesday of the same week and Edward Mendez was acting on a hunch. He was driving toward the Coney Island section of Brooklyn; to the amusement park that housed one of the biggest fun houses on the east coast. His girlfriend, Yolanda, was sitting next to him. She finished her morning practice session and was taking the afternoon off.

-I've never even been to Coney Island.

-I used to go there all the time in the summer, to the beach, mostly, when I was a kid.

-Wasn't it very crowded?

-Not if you got there early enough and knew the right spot to go to. I spent most of my time in the water, anyway.

-And, Edward, this fun house...do you think that this killer is hiding out there?

-If he isn't, then there's something in there that Missy Wingate and John and Erica Mills shouldn't have seen.

-It must have been pretty bad to cost them their lives.

-I'll say! Look. You can see the parachute jump from here.

-You'd never get me up there.

Edward laughed.

-It was the one ride I was afraid to go on. And, by the way, just to warn you, there's gonna' be at least one civilian squad car blocking the fun house exit.

-I don't mind at all. But, Edward, is the park still open this time of year? It's past Labor Day.

-It's gonna' be open 'til the end of the month. It's been such a damned chilly summer that business hasn't been so great; so, they're keeping things open for a few extra weeks.

-Am I coming in with you? Better say yes.

-You bet, but don't budge from my side. I mean it, Yolanda.

-Don't worry, I won't.

-The two of us going in will look a lot less suspicious.

Yolanda nodded.

-It will. But-

-Uh-huh?

-Are we looking for something or someone?

-For my money, I hope it turns out to be someone. I'd like to wrap up this case.

-So, we're maybe looking for a bogeyman in a spook house?

-You could put it that way; but, this bogeyman kills for real and drives getaway cars, too.

The sun hadn't reached its peak in the sky, but it shone overhead against a cloudless sky. Edward and Yolanda walked up to the Fun House ticket booth where he purchased two tickets. They went through the turn-stile and were greeted by a friendly ticket taker who guided them into the circular two seater car. He placed the safety chain across the opening of the car.

-Have a good time, folks.

-Thank you.

-Ready, baby?

-I think so.

-Stay in the car and don't leave my side.

The car started up and moved along its steel track that had a lot of twists and turns. The car "plowed" through a set of painted double doors, but some sunlight filtered in through the "cracks" of the ceiling making one appreciate the sunlight even more. In an endless circular path, Yolanda and Edward's car meandered past ghouls in cages who peered out at them as hysterical laughter and screams permeated the tunnel.

Edward drew his gun and kept glancing from side to side with an occasional glance overhead. At one point, the P. I. stood up thinking that he saw a passing shadow. or was it a make believe phantom? Was it his imagination or part of the amusement or was it real?

Yolanda was fascinated by the play of lights: garish reds, pinks, greens and yellows – flashing on and off. She thought she saw the shadow of a man peering out from one of the ghosts' cages.

-Edward?

-What is it?

-I can't be sure, but a shadow keeps appearing. It just doesn't fit in with the other displays. It's too subtle. You have to be quick to notice it.

Edward gripped his gun.

-I saw it, too. Thanks for the confirmation.

Without warning, their car jerked to a halt. There were other patrons in the fun house and a lot of shouting went up.

-What the hell's goin' on?

-Hey, man, we're like stuck in here.

-Get the damned ride goin' already.

And, in Edward's car...

-Yolanda, hold on to my arm and don't lose sight of me. At least the lights in the displays haven't gone out.

-I know. It's like a panorama of electric pinks and yellows.

-Uh-huh.

Edward stood up in the car and tried to catch hold of that "shadow" that both he and his girlfriend spotted. Whatever it was, he knew it was coming for the two of them. His eyes had already grown accustomed to the dark, but the glare of the lights distorted everything. A clicking noise caught his attention.

-Edward! Oh, my God! A hand just undid the chain on the car. It ran off in that direction. It was that same shadow of a man — that phantom.

Edward spun around and fired in the direction that Yolanda was pointing to. Some of the patrons in the other cars screamed. Edward cried out.

-Everyone, keep down!

A hand reached over the back of the car and touched Yolanda. She screamed. Edward turned about and fired. He heard a muffled cry.

-Got the bastard. You okay, baby?

-I think so. But, what about him?

He looked over the top of the car. No one was there; but, he heard someone's footsteps. Edward called out.

-Give it up. You're through. Don't make me shoot, again.

The P. I. turned right and then left aiming his gun in every conceivable direction. Yolanda glanced to her right and a gaunt face was staring right at her. She screamed and Edward fired point blank just grazing the thing's temple. It staggered back a few feet and fell to the ground.

Edward jumped out of the car.

-Stay put.

-Not on your life. I'm coming with you.

-Come on, then.

The two of them approached the fallen "shadow" who in fact was a man. Edward still had his gun drawn and was ready to fire. He wasn't about to take any chances. The figure on the floor turned over to face them. He held something in his hand, but neither Edward nor Yolanda could make it out.

The figure on the floor spoke in a surprisingly lucid voice.

-I'm still alive, just. Your first bullet hit the mark. You're a pretty good shot, shamus. I'm dying, but not fast enough. The medics just might reach me before I take my last breath. And, by the way, I was only trying to scare you. I don't kill when I don't have to.

Standing over him with his gun drawn, Edward spoke to the man.

-Who are you?

-Josef Antonio's henchman. When he couldn't do the job himself, he sent me out. The bastard kept me on a leash...always promising to pay up, but he never did.

-You killed John and Erica Mills?

-No. He did. And he bumped off the fat woman, too. I don't kill that way. I make it short and quick.

-How? Tell me how he did it.

-I was wrong- I'm not gonna' make it 'til the medics get here.

-How did he kill them?

-I can't tell you that.

-You might as well.

-No. It's too terrible. And, if I do live...there are worse things than the electric chair.

-This Josef Antonio, who the hell was he?

-Told me he was two thousand years old. I didn't believe him. But, I was a crack shot and could do execution style killings.

-And, where the hell do you come from?

-Just a kid from the slums, really. Antonio picked me up when I tried robbing him in a downtown bar. Christ! The fucking pain, man! You got me good. You're not such a bad shot yourself.

Yolanda tugged at Edward's arm.

-Edward, he's dying. Look at his eyes.

In spite of herself, Yolanda felt sorry for this young man.

-Look, his eyes are starting to glaze over.

-Why'd he kill them? Why?

-They saw Antonio jump off the car and head into my hiding place: that young couple and the fat lady. They saw too much, so he came up from behind them and...like it was part of the ride. That young guy was real ticked off. The ladies were just plain scared. And...and, I'm real sorry about the boy.

-You oughta' be. You tried gunning down Teresa Farmer.

-Yeah. But, she was a chick who could look-

He stopped talking and dropped dead.

Edward bent down to see what he had in his hand. It was a glass cap off a perfume bottle. Against his better judgment, he picked it up and sniffed it. He handed it to Yolanda .

-Take a whiff.

-Nice. Like rose petals. And, I'm sure it's quite expensive, probably French.

-Hmm. He doesn't strike me as the type to wear a woman's perfume.

-It could have been part of Antonio's disguise as a woman.

-You're right, Girl Friday. That makes sense. But, why is he carrying it around with him?

-I think I know why. Maybe, their relationship was more intimate that it should have been.

Chapter Seven
Thursday, September 16, 1948
Dinner at Mom's Place

IT WAS a late Thursday afternoon and Edward and Yolanda were having dinner at his mother's place in Brooklyn Heights. Mrs. Mendez and her daughters Nella, Dottie, and Victoria were gathered in the living room with the P. I. and his girlfriend who were sitting next to each other on the sofa. Nella was sitting with them and Mrs. Mendez, Dottie, and Victoria each sat in an armchair. The sun was about to set as a ray of light receded across the living room rug.

Everyone in the room had been briefed by Edward on his most recent case and each woman had her own opinion. Mrs. Mendez started the conversation.

-Edward?

-Yes, mother? Good dinner, by the way.

-Thank you. This Josef Antonio claimed to live during the time of Christ?

-He did. And, just how he did that, we'll probably never know.

-It's a pity that he had to be killed. Many secrets must have died with him. Imagine...an eye witness to the crucifixion.

Yolanda's eyes were wide and bright.

-Mrs. Mendez, he might have even witnessed the resurrection. Can you imagine such a thing?

Dottie laughed.

-In a word: wow!

-I hate to throw cold water on you, ladies, but Josef Antonio was a cold blooded killer. He got what was coming to him. Don't feel too sorry for him. He must have tapped into some dark Sumerian secret of the occult. We're better off not knowing.

Dottie spoke up.

-I wonder if father knew him. I'll bet he did.

-Beats me.

Victoria asked her question.

-Was he some kind of vampire, Eddie?

-If you mean, Victoria, did he have to kill people to live: yes. We call them murderers.

-But, Eddie, he was the one who killed that couple out in Long Island and that woman in Brooklyn.

-He was the one all right, Dottie. But, how he did it, we don't know just yet.

Nella put down her coffee cup.

-Why didn't he just shoot the Mills couple and Missy Wingate or send his henchman out to do it?

Edward pointed his cigarette at his sister.

-Good question, Nella. That's just what I was thinking along with Sgt. Rayno and Lt. Donovan.

Victoria was stirring her coffee deep in thought. Edward smiled at his beautiful sister and continued to answer Nella's question.

-The police are taking apart that fun house and autopsies are being done on both men. Now, those results oughta' be interesting, especially the one on Antonio.

-A couple of perverts, if you ask me.

Edward laughed.

-I was just waiting for you to say that, Dottie. They were a couple of deviants, all right.

Mrs. Mendez spoke up.

-I find the case of Missy Wingate and the Mills couple intriguing and even frightening. Edward, I think that should be your number one priority. If this Josef Antonio was able to perpetrate such a ghastly crime, others may also share that terrible ability. And, I do have a theory as to why it was done.

Yolanda addressed the matriarch.

-What's your theory, Mrs. Mendez? And, I also find it frightening.

-They were part of some kind of macabre experiment; subject testing, I believe it's called. The Nazis were infamous for conducting such experiments.

Yolanda sat forward.

-Yes! That's what I was thinking, too. But, experiments for what? I'm not so sure that I want to know.

Mrs. Mendez let out a sigh.

-I wish I knew, my dear. We must leave that to the police and Edward.

-As soon as the medics are done, we should have a clearer picture of what we're up against.

Dottie looked hard at her brother.

-And, what exactly does that mean? Isn't it over with both men dead?

Edward shook his head in the negative.

-I doubt it, sis. I've got that P. I. gut feeling that we've just seen the tip of the iceberg. Mr. Antonio just might have a cadre of followers; that type usually does.

-I hope you're wrong, brother mine. And, look who just walked in.

Dottie scooped up her tabby cat, Stripes.

-I was wondering where you were.

Edward spoke to his mother.

And, I was wondering about my eldest sister, Catrina. How is she? Has she made any progress?

Mrs. Mendez looked grim.

-As well as can be expected, I imagine. She never leaves her room and barely utters a word to anyone. Most of the time, she simply stares into space.

Dottie couldn't pass that one up.

-Lucky us. I don't mean to be cruel, but there really is no reason why she can't get out of bed and come downstairs. Her face is scarred, but not that bad. A little make-up would go a long way.

-My daughter's vanity won't permit it. But, why she doesn't speak...it worries me.

Nella had some information to offer.

-Mother, when Catrina was in the hospital, the head nurse said that she had two visitors: an elderly man and woman. And, she heard voices, my sister's voice was amongst them.

-Who were these visitors, Nella?

-I've no idea. Why not ask Catrina?

-I shall. That's most curious.

-Mother? Yolanda, Nella and I are going to a séance tomorrow.

-Indeed. Isn't there a solar eclipse due tomorrow morning?

-I think so.

-Be careful, Edward. Remember what happened at our last séance.

Yolanda shivered at the memory.

-I'll never forget it.

-Eddie? Not inviting me and Victoria?

Edward smiled and waved his just lit cigarette about in the air.

-I was just about to, Dottie. I don't think Marlena would mind. She loves company.

-Marlena Lake, Edward?

-That's right. Has her notoriety reached even you, mother?

-Your father knew of her. She's a woman not to be trusted. But, she's talented or so your father thought.

-Resourceful and determined, that's for damned sure.

-And ruthless. She's an expert manipulator, Mrs. Mendez. And, her hobby is collecting people.

-I like you, Yolanda. You're perceptive and straight forward.

Edward looked over at Dottie and Victoria.

-Well, ladies, are you game?

Dottie put down Stripes.

-I'll say! You can count me in. How about it, Victoria?

-You can count me out. And, Eddie, please be careful.

Dottie pressed her sister.

-Oh, Victoria, come. It'll be fun. We'll look after you.

Victoria smiled sweetly at her sister.

-No. Thank you. You weren't here for our last séance. I was.

Mrs. Mendez waited for her daughters to be asleep. Patiently, she knitted in her favorite armchair in the living room. The grandfather clock was ticking away and that was a comfort to the old matriarch. She could hear Dottie getting ready for bed. And, was that her bedroom door closing? Yes. Of course it was.

She put down her knitting and climbed the stairs to her eldest daughter's bedroom. Should she knock first? No. Her other daughters might hear and they were sure to be curious. As quietly as she could, Mrs. Mendez opened the door to Catrina's bedroom. The room was impeccably clean and neat with not a speck of dust on any surface or in any corner. How did her daughter manage it?

-Catrina, are you awake?

No answer.

-Catrina? Please, answer me if you are.

-I'm awake, mother. Please, come in.

Mrs. Mendez entered the bedroom and closed the door. She was about to flip on the light switch but her daughter stopped her.

-Please, don't. This light by the bed is sufficient enough.

-How are you, dear?

-I'm quite well. Please, sit down on the chair next to my bed. I'm glad you came to me.

-Of course. We're all very concerned about you.

Mrs. Isabelle Mendez sat down and looked at her eldest daughter. Her face was scarred, but the scars seemed to be healing to some extent. Her hair had grown back in, but the rest of her body had been more severely injured.

-Are my sisters concerned for me?

-Of course. Victoria and Nella constantly ask about you.

-And, Dottie?

-In her own way, she's concerned, as well. Catrina? Why do you not speak to anyone? What is the matter? Please, tell me.

Catrina evaded her mother's question.

-In the hospital, I had visitors.

-I meant to ask you about that. Nella mentioned as much.

-I thought that you might. You know them. Nathalie Montaigne and Werner Hoffman.

-Indeed. And, what did they want of you?

-Information, of course.

-What kind of information could you possibly give them?

-News of the anti-Christ.

-There is no anti-Christ. You know this as well as I do. Did they believe you?

-I don't know. I had to tell them something.

-Catrina? You have escaped death…your fate, if you would. I'm asking you to be grateful. Try to be. The eldest daughter was to be sacrificed in order for the bloodline to continue. It will continue now and you can live.

-Edward will continue it.

-Yes. And, his girlfriend, Yolanda, is also versed in the occult. I like her and so should you. You must make an effort to be more congenial.

-I was annoyed with her at the seance. Maybe, I even envied her. I can admit to that now. I've never liked strangers coming into the house

-Neither do I; but one must make exceptions.

-Will she forgive me my rudeness?

-I'm sure she will. She is an ally. We can make good use of her.

-I'll make the effort. But, Edward…is he receptive to his inheritance? to father's inheritance? A pity that he never knew father.

-He's struggling with it at present. He'll come around.

There was the most subtle of sounds just outside Catrina's bedroom. Mrs. Mendez smiled.

-Someone is trying to overhear what she shouldn't. It's probably Dottie. No matter. We're concluded for now.

Mrs. Mendez rose from her chair.

-And, young lady, you will come down to breakfast tomorrow morning. And, try to be pleasant.

-I'm almost looking forward to it, mother.

Chapter Eight
Friday, September 17, 1948
Park Avenue Seance

FRIDAY MORNING and Edward and Yolanda were at the P. I.'s office. Nella and Dottie were going to meet up with them at the address that Marlena had given to Edward.

The results of the autopsy were in and they revealed no abnormalities in either man except for a high level of cranial fluid in Josef Antonio's brain stem. What this meant was still to be determined. Autopsies on Missy Wingate and the Mills couple were completed. Dr. Aster and Dr., Ingram were in consultation at that very moment. Edward was at his desk expecting their call.

Yolanda sat at the portable table where Nella did the accounts.

-Edward, what did the police find at the fun house?

-A bunker of sorts in the back room: cans of food, a sleeping bag and some clothing.

-That's all? No lab equipment or chemicals? I'm surprised. I thought a mad scientist would have a fully equipped lab with a skeleton hanging in the corner and one of those electric machines that shoot lightning bolts.

Edward laughed.

-You'd think so. And, why I'm laughing, I don't know. And, we'd better get going. Don't want to be late for Marlena's séance.

The phone rang.

-Edward Mendez.

-Mendez, Dr. Ingram here. Got a minute?

Dr. Ingram didn't wait for an answer.

-We've been working on a false premise, shamus.

-What the hell does that mean?

Edward didn't like Dr. Claire Ingram and didn't mind letting her know.

-Just this: nothing was injected into the three victims – Wingate and the Mills – but and, I must stress this, something was drawn out via a hypodermic.

-Like what?

-Cranial fluid from their brain stems. The brain stems on all three victims were withered; dry as a Sahara sand dune.

-So, that's what aged them to the point of death?

-Yes.

-But, why? What the hell did he do with the fluid? Could he do anything with the damn fluid?

-That's one question. We've got to run a few more tests. That cranial fluid may have been used in concert with something else.

-Like what?

-Blood or a chemical we're not familiar with. It could be the key to the proverbial fountain of youth. Men have killed for less.

Edward was forced to agree with her.

Later that Friday morning at Park Avenue and 30th St., Edward and Yolanda were standing in the lobby of that particular building.   Edward pushed the "up" button and they waited for the elevator to arrive.

-Edward, now that we're here, I can say this. I'm surprised that you agreed to come at all.

-So am I, baby. I don't like seances. They open doorways to God-only-knows-where.

-Did Marlena say why she's conducting one? I'll bet she didn't.

-I didn't ask. But- well, it's been months since I've spoken to her. I get the feeling she's ticked off at me. Can't say I blame her.

-She's ticked off at the world. And, she's probably up to something, knowing her.

Edward took out a cigarette, but didn't light up.

-I just had a thought. Just maybe, she's not conducting this little séance.

-Then, who is?

-Beats the hell out of me.

The elevator arrived.

-When the soul is released upon death, is there pain or simply utter blackness? Have we lived this life to merely face oblivion in the end?

-Mother? Are we having a philosophical moment?

-A reflective moment. Do you know, Susan, that I am close to being a semi-recluse? My books and research satisfy my wants, for the most part.

-A recluse, mother? Are you serious? And, what about collecting people?

-Dear Susan, you do know me, don't you?

-Like a book.

Susan looked about the large room.

-And, where is our hostess?

Marlena made a face.

-Gazing into her vanity mirror, no doubt. Miss Linda Kawano, an Asian beauty, who hasn't aged a day in the twenty-five years that I've known her. You've never met her face-to-face have you, Susan?

-No, as a matter of fact, I haven't. I have spoken with Miss Kawano on the phone several times, though. She speaks perfect English.

-Why thank you, Susan. And, I'm glad you two ladies are occupying yourselves with conversation.

Linda Kawano entered the ornately furnished living room. Her long, black hair reached down to her waist and her slim figure was encased in a midnight blue mandarin dress. Her face was both striking and flawless in its porcelain-like beauty. Many years ago, she had been a prostitute and had even dabbled in portraiture of a kind to supplement her diminished income. She approached her guests.

-Susan? So nice to meet you at long last. May I get you ladies a drink?

-A bourbon on the rocks.

-Just ginger-ale for me, Miss Kawano.

-Linda, please. And, you should both gaze out the window. The eclipse is due to start soon. Maybe, you can even spy our other guests approaching.

Marlena and Susan moved closer to the window.

-I don't see them, mother; but, I've never met Edward's two sister. Have you?

Marlena evaded the question.

-Look. There's Edward and Yolanda. They've just entered the building. I've got quite a bit to say to Mr. Mendez.

Marlena turned back to face her hostess who was offering a tray of drinks.

-Thank you, my dear.

-Susan? Your ginger-ale?

-Oh. Thank you. We've just spotted two of your guests.

-Excellent. They may be a few minutes. The elevators in this building are slow.

Marlena addressed Miss Kawano.

-They still have time. Linda, have you ever witnessed a solar eclipse?

-Only once before have I witnessed one. I liked it. The darkness appealed to me and the sound...there was sound...an ethereal vibration. You could hear it only if you listened for it. It came from the void between the earth and the moon and it spoke of death.

-Are you afraid of death, my dear?

-No. Only of growing old which I will never experience.

That statement made Marlena smile. The ice in her glass tinkled and melted into the alcohol. Marlena took a sip of her drink and waited for the other guests to arrive.

-Marlena?

-Yes, Linda?

-Thank you for inviting Mr. Mendez. I'm very anxious to meet this private investigator.

-Edward Mendez is a very resourceful young man. He is also gifted with certain occult powers that he's not all that enthusiastic about. His father, Manuel Mendez, was greatly respected in occult circles. You might have heard of him.

-I knew of his father. He was reputed to be a great magician and even feared.

-Precisely why I admire the man.

Susan joined the conversation.

-His girlfriend is an amateur ice skater who just competed in the Olympics. She's pretty intelligent and open-minded. I can't speak for his sisters.

The doorbell rang.

-Excuse me, ladies.

Miss Kawano went to open the door.

Marlena turned to her daughter who was now gazing out the window. Susan touched the window pane and drew back. It was so cold that it chilled her entire body.

-What is it, Susan?

-Is it so cold outside? I don't remember it being that cold.

-It was rather chilly when we arrived.

-Chilly but not freezing. Mother, what is it? You're worried about something, aren't you?

Marlena didn't get a chance to answer her daughter's question. Edward and Yolanda entered the living room with Nella and Dottie Mendez who had caught up with them downstairs in the lobby.

After all the introductions had been made, Marlena wasted no time in cornering Edward.

-So, where have you been all these past months, dear boy? Too busy for even a phone call? I'm quite angry with you.

Edward was ready for this.

-Earning my bread and butter, Marlena. I don't come from money. I have to work for a living. And, my last case took a lot out of me.

-Yes. The Angel Ulysses Correa case: most intriguing. And, I've been reading the papers about your rather spectacular exploits in regards to that case. You're building quite a reputation for yourself. We must speak about it at length. But, about money and having to earn a living…that needn't be the case with my help, Edward.

-My police contacts have helped me out…a lot. And, my "exploits" have been pretty interesting ones. Something you might be interested…or involved in, Marlena.

-You just made either a statement or an accusation. I know who you refer to: Mr. Josef Antonio.

Edward raised his drink.

-Why am I not surprised. And, just how well did you know him?

-He was my house guest these past months. He came to me about the time of the Angel Correa case.

-You've gotta' be kidding me, lady. And, you knew-

-No. I knew nothing of his current crimes. Never would I condone the killing of innocent people, especially a young boy. Had he returned to my house, I would have notified the police.

Edward swallowed the remainder of his scotch and soda. He shook his head.

-You skate on real thin ice, Marlena. It's so thin that Yolanda wouldn't skate on it. What about his past crimes? Did you know about them? Level with me.

-Not specifically.

-You just had this general idea that the guy was a murdering deviant who'd do anything to keep on living — if you can call it that. That's called living real close to the edge of the cliff. You could be considered an accessory; do you know that?

-Dear boy, it does add a dash of excitement to one's life. But, that's not why I invited you here. I must speak to you about something infinitely more important.

Edward looked her straight and hard in the eye.

-Like what? This séance we're about to hold?

Marlena pointed a finger at the P. I.

-And, you had enough good sense to join me here today. Remember, Edward, you and I share many secrets and that includes your little girlfriend over there.

-Talking about secrets, there's someone who'd like to meet you.

-Who, pray tell?

-Professor Frank Moreland. He's taken over Professor Lange's position at the foundation.

-I know. I make it a point to keep up on these things. You mentioned me to him?

-As matter of fact, I did. Hope you don't mind.

-In what context was I mentioned?

-It was about my loss of memory for those few hours back in April of last year.

-When we have time, you must tell me all about it.

-He said I was a "time jumper."

-I actually know what he meant by that. We must discuss this further-

Their hostess caught their attention.

-Look, everyone, the eclipse is beginning.

Everyone in the room could feel a vibration in the air as the shadow of the eclipse enveloped the city. In the street below, people stopped and gazed skyward. A silence gripped the populace as the immense shadow spread across the metropolis plunging it into the abyss of darkness. As it grew darker, the vibration – or was it the presence of God? – pierced the soul of Edward Mendez. He heard it...the deafening music of three worlds grazing the soul of each other...the earth and the heavens in conflict. The sun was now almost hidden by the moon. And, then, Edward noticed it.

-Look. The moon is just below the sun and...

-Yes. Even if it were in perfect alignment, it wouldn't be a complete solar eclipse. Edward, this is what I feared.

Miss Kawano spoke.

-The eclipse will be over in a few minutes. We should begin to get ready for the séance. If no one objects, I will be conducting it. But, please, everyone, help yourselves to another drink before we start.

Miss Kawano went into her bedroom and shut the door.

Nella and Susan were on the sofa discussing the very cool summer that had just passed.

Nella Mendez decided quite quickly that she liked Susan Broder. The young girl's intelligence and easy manner spoke for themselves. The feeling was mutual on Susan's side.

-It was growing chillier by the moment when Dottie and I came in.

-I know. When I touched the window pane before, my whole body went cold.

-It's been a very cool summer. I don't know what to make of it.

Susan smiled.

-I think my mother might have a theory about that. But, then, again she's never short of theories.

-My brother, Edward, has spoken of her and you, Susan. He admires you.

-I noticed that you didn't mention my mother in that sentence. Mind you, I understand. You either like my mother or despise her: there's no middle ground.

-I'm sure Edward doesn't despise her.

-Does he trust her, Nella?

-Let's just say that he's wary of her motives.

-I like you, Nella Mendez. We must have lunch together sometime next week. .

-I'd love it.

Dottie and Yolanda were still looking at the now almost completed eclipse.

-Awesome. It really gives you a sense of the universe.

-Doesn't it? I love to read about astronomy and the stars.

-You're kind of a star yourself, Yolanda. Good job at the Nationals. We were all glued to the radio.

-Thank you. But, I was a little disappointed that I didn't win.

-But, you were the first to pull off…what do you call it? A double-axel jump?

-That's right. That was thrilling and it got a big applause.

-I got a feeling you're gonna' win this time. I've got my brother Edward's P. I. gut feeling.

Marlena steered Edward into the far corner of the living room.

-Linda may come out at any moment.

She asked Edward a rhetorical question.

-Did you just witness what happened in the heavens?

-What did just happen? Explain it to me, please. I'm no scientist.

-What you witnessed could be the beginning of the end. Mark those words, Edward.

Miss Kawano came back into the room.

-If everyone is ready, we'll proceed.

Everyone found a place at the round table that had been set up. Edward, Yolanda, Nella, Dottie, Susan, Marlena, and Miss Kawano next to Edward.

Miss Kawano gave the instructions.

-We must touch hands and focus our minds upon the eclipse that will soon end. Who will come to us? Does one dare speak his name? Listen to the pressure in the air for it speaks your name. The silence within the silence is deafening.

The group of assembled people was like a pinpoint of light in an abyss. Each person at that table felt suspended in mid-air.

Again, Miss Kawano spoke.

-Will no one speak to those of us assembled?

A clap of thunder startled everyone. The clear day had turned dark with thunderheads. Lightning streaked across the Manhattan skyline and the rain came pouring down.

A voice was heard at the table...a voice coming from Edward Mendez. He was now a spectator who'd been dislodged from his own body. The voice spoke.

-I cannot help you.

Miss Kawano responded in a panicky voice.

-You must! You wouldn't have come to us otherwise.

-My powers of understanding are gone.

-Tell us your name.

-I? I am one for whom he broke the sacred law.

This was not the person Miss Kawano wanted to contact.

-What are you telling us? Who are you? Our leader is gone and I must know who will replace him.

Marlena looked pointedly at Susan who understood.

-I tell you that I still live.

-You're alive? How? Tell me the secret. I'm begging you.

-I live.

Miss Kawano was frustrated. She wanted to end the séance, but couldn't.

-Your name – what is your name?

-Lazarus.

-Are you that Lazarus who was brought back from the dead? Are you that Lazarus whose body lay interred and stinking in its coffin?

-He condemned me.

-I understand. Where are you now?

-In the purgatory between heaven and hell.

Miss Kawano was getting more angry.

-But, you just said that you still live.

-In that phantasmic realm.

A lightning bolt struck and a window burst open. Edward came to his senses and the séance came to an end.

Yolanda touched her boyfriend's forearm. He gave out a sigh and turned to face her.

-What the hell just happened? It's like I was staring down from the ceiling at all of you. I cold even see myself.

-You were the chosen medium. Lazarus spoke through you.

-Lazarus? You don't mean-

-Yes. Lazarus from the Bible who was raised from the dead.

Miss Kawano ran over to the open window to latch it shut.

-It's pouring rain outside. Ladies and Edward, please help yourselves to the drinks table. Very soon, I must ask you all to leave.

-I could go for a scotch. Nella, care to join me?

-As a matter of fact, Dottie, yes. Edward, are you all right?

-I'm fine, sis

-Cone on, Nella. Let's have one for the road.

-I'm right behind you, Dottie.

The two sisters went over to the drinks table and helped themselves. Marlena and Susan joined them.

-Miss Kawano?

-Yes, Edward? And, please call me Linda.

-Okay.

The P. I. rubbed his forehead. He had a real bad headache.

-So, what was the point of this séance? If you don't mind my asking.

Miss Kawano smiled at her handsome, Latin guest.

-Don't you know? Why to meet you, of course. It was a special lure for a special man.

Edward took out a cigarette and lit up. He and Yolanda were the only one still seated at the table.

-Why?

-Until today, I knew of you; but, I didn't know you personally. How can I phrase it? You hadn't yet entered my sphere of consciousness.

Marlena walked over from the drinks table with her bourbon on the rocks in hand.

-Well said, my dear. And, you've seen for yourself how talented this shamus is.

-I was impressed. I know him now. He has fulfilled my expectations. Edward? There's an ashtray on the end table that you can use. It's right over there.

-I'll get it for you.

That was Yolanda who had decided that she didn't like Miss Kawano.

-Linda, do you need my services as a private investigator?

-No. I have far more interesting plans for you.

-Want to tell me what they are?

-Not now. Not yet.

-Suit yourself. Marlena? You made a pretty dramatic statement a little while ago. You want to explain it to me now?

-Not here, dear boy. I may still be wrong. I'll get in touch with you soon. Sunday. Yes. This Sunday come to my town house for dinner and don't be late. We'll discuss it then.

Yolanda smiled sweetly at Marlena.

-Am I invited, too?

-Of course. That goes without saying. I can make use of you.

Miss Kawano was about to say something, but thought better of it.

Chapter Nine

Saturday, September 18, 1948
Hotel Showdown

IT WAS early Saturday morning. The rain had ended at midnight.. Edward was let into his office building by the night watchman who was just getting off duty. It was only 5 A. M. and barely light outside. The P. I. had had a restless night; couldn't quite drift off into a deep sleep; just some light fitful snatches of rest filled with incoherent dreams. He forced himself out of bed with a splitting headache that even his morning cigarette couldn't help. Yolanda was asleep and he didn't want to disturb her. He got dressed but didn't bother to shave. What the hell for? He grabbed his jacket and Fedora and was about to leave.

　　-Edward? Leaving without saying goodbye? You could at least kiss me goodbye.

　　He put down his Fedora and walked over to the bed.

　　-Sorry, baby. Didn't want to wake you up. Get back to sleep. You've got time before practice.

　　-No. I'll get up now. I'm wide awake. Can I get you a cup of coffee?

-No, thanks, baby. I want to get to the office. I'll get a take-out downtown. Don't let any strangers in. I mean it.

Edward kissed his girlfriend goodby and left for the office.

Yolanda put the coffee on and took a quick shower. When she got out, she poured herself a coffee and got dressed. In a few minutes, she was ready to leave for practice. Yes. She had everything she needed: ice skates, costume and, of course, her handbag. She was running a little late and had to hurry.

The doorbell rang and without thinking she went to answer it.

Edward Mendez, P. I. headed downtown to sort through the notes he'd made of his recent case. On his way to the office, he stopped off at his favorite delicatessen to get a container of coffee and a B.L.T. sandwich. The coffee was freshly brewed and the aroma of the bacon almost healed his stubborn headache.

He rang for the elevator and waited. He'd have to operate it himself because the lift man wouldn't be in until 10 A.M....so where was the elevator? Someone must have gotten here ahead of him and taken it up. He gritted his teeth and was about to begin the ten floor climb to his office when he heard the elevator coming down. It reached ground level and the accordion doors opened. Jack Marino was operating it. Edward couldn't have been more surprised.

-Hello, Jack Marino. We've been worried about you. What gives?

-Hello, Mr. Mendez. I'll take you up.

Edward noticed the worried look on the young boy's face...worry or fright? Hard to tell. And, the teenager was sweating.

The P. I. stepped into the elevator.

-Is everything all right with you, Jack? You're not looking too good. And, I'm not being mean.

-That's a hard one to answer. Mind if I take a pass?

-I'm not trying to pry. But, we have been worried. Even Adam, our mailman, was asking about you. You're liked here. You know that, don't you?

-I-

-What is it? You want to say something? You look a little different. You're not in any kind of trouble, are you?

-Here's your floor, Mr. Mendez.

Jack released the elevator door and it slid open. Edward stepped out into the dark corridor. He didn't see Jack Marino reaching down to grab a hidden blackjack. He felt the blow to the back of his head just before he lost consciousness.

Edward woke up in a dark and musty room. He hands and feet were bound with rope and his mouth was gagged. He was tied to a straight back wooden chair. He opened his eyes and couldn't see a thing; but, he felt the closeness of his confinement. A closet. It had to be a clothes closet of sorts. He peered upward and could just make out some wire coat hangers. He tried pulling at the ropes on his wrists. Tight. The ropes were burning his flesh as he tried getting loose. He was about to try for his feet when the door opened and a figure of a man walked in. He closed the door and turned on the overhead light bulb.

Jack Marino took the gag off of Edward's mouth.

-You bastard. I should've known something was up. And, I turned my back on you. Christ! I oughta' have my license revoked.

-They sent me in to talk to you.

-Who's "they?" And, why the hell am I here and where's "here?" Answer me, boy!

-They're a cult, Mr. Mendez. You killed their leader and his left-hand man.

-You mean Antonio and that bogeyman from the fun house.

-Right.

-That wasn't a question. And, why not just bump me off like Patty Kilmeade or the Sandersons? Your people are real good at that.

-They want to induct you.

-What the hell are you telling me? Induct me into what?

-Make you one of them.

-Are you one of them, Jack?

-Not yet. I had to bring your here first.

Edward grinned.

-So, I'm the price of admission, huh?

-I'm real sorry, Mr. Mendez.

-I'll bet! What are they, Jack? Are they like what Angel Correa was or closer to what Antonio was? I want answers.

-Not like Angel. No. They feed on fluid from people's brain stems. I don't really understand it.

-My God! And, that's what happened to Missy Wingate and the Mills couple?

-Yes. But-

-What? Tell me, Jack. This inductee had a right to know.

-The fluid has to be mixed with blood or some other chemical. It's how Antonio stayed alive for so long.

-Brain vampires, huh?

He had to keep Jack talking. The ropes around his ankles were starting to come loose.

-What makes you think I'll join?

-They've got your girlfriend.

-What? You're bluffing me, man. You'd better be.

-As soon as you left her apartment, they went in and took her. She's here, Mr. Mendez, in another room...over in the next room. They haven't harmed her.

-Where exactly is she? Tell me.

And, why was Jack telling him all this? Edward thought he knew why. And, just a little more and he'd have his feet free.

-In their meeting room right across the hall. She's okay, but plenty scared. I tried to talk to her, but they wouldn't let me.

Edward had his feet freed.

-This is there revenge, huh?

-I guess. But, they chose you especially. She chose you.

-"She?"

-Miss Kawano. She's pretty much in charge here. Well, her and Kenneth Ng. He was in your building the other week. I think he broke into your office and took some of your files.

So, that was the real reason for the séance. The whole thing had been a setup to feel him out and see what occult stuff he was made of. And, Edward knew the files that Jack was talking about: the atom bomb blasts. But, did Jack know?

-What did they take out of my office?

-I don't know. Something in your files that he needed to get his hands on, I think. They don't tell me much.

-They don't trust you, pal.

-They want me to bring you inside.

-Who the hell's stopping you?

-I'm real sorry I've gotta' do this to you.

-Blow a person's head off? Condemn some poor slob to die of old age seventy years before his time? You want this, Jack? I can't believe it. You're condemning yourself to a living hell.

-Not that part of it.

-Then, why, Jack? Tell me why.

-Money. I needed money. I don't wanna' be poor all my life. I don't wanna' live in a one room roach infested tenement with babies screaming all night...and me being picked on.

-Jack, let Yolanda go. I don't think your heart is in this. It's not too late to get out of it with clean hands. You help me and I'll help you. Trust me.

The rope around his wrists were loose just a little.

Jack lifted Edward up by his shoulders. The P. I. braced his feet to the floor and shoved Jack hard against the closet wall. Edward pinned him there for just a second and, then, shoved him to the floor and gave him a hard kick to the head with his elbow.

Edward worked his hands loose and, then, tied up the now unconscious Jack. Crouching down, he opened the closet door just a crack. What he saw was an empty hallway with a lot of debris in it. He was about to close the closet door when he spotted his shoulder holster hanging on the closet's wooden pole. He grabbed it and checked for ammunition – no bullets! Well, at lest, he could use it as a hand weapon.

Edward heard voices in the room across the hallway. He stepped out into the hallway closing the closet door. He walked over to the door from where the voices were coming and pressed his ear to it. There had to be at least three or four people in there; but the P. I. couldn't make out any words.

Did he dare risk looking in? He was saved from making that decision as he was grabbed by both arms and shoved into a large, dark room. There were four people sitting in a semi-circle about a rectangular coffee table. A tall man stood up and addressed him.

-Mr. Mendez. Welcome. My name is Kenneth Ng. You've already met Miss Kawano. The man to your immediate left is Hans Becker and to your immediate right Freda Becker, his sister. They've taken the liberty of escorting you into our lair.

Edward recognized these people from the police composite sketches. The only person not known to him was Mr. Kenneth Ng.

Edward took a shot at Hans Becker.

-Lucky you, pal. Your sister's too damned ugly to be anyone's girlfriend.

-Should I break this shamus' arm, Mr. Ng? I don't like his insolence or his insults.

-No. You may not, Mr. Becker. Mr. Mendez will soon be inducted and most complacent.

-Don't count on it. Where the hell is this place? And, Mr. Ng, tell this bulldog to take his fucking hands off me. Now!

-Let him go, Mr. Becker.

Edward was let go. He staggered forward a few feet.

Linda Kawano spoke to him and there was a distinct hardness in her voice that hadn't been there at the séance.

-There is no escape for you, Edward Mendez. Cooperate and we'll allow your pretty girlfriend to live. You don't have any choice; that is, if she means anything to you. You wouldn't want her to age prematurely, would you?

Edward forced a calm that he didn't feel. As he took in the other members of this cult a petite and very pretty strawberry blonde was smiling up at him.

-Mr. Mendez, I'm Jennifer Caswell. You can sit next to me while you get yourself acclimated. I won't bite. Promise.

Edward sat down. This girl had the perfect doll's figure that was pretty close to perfection. Everything about her spoke of one thing: money. The material and cut of her clothes and even the black high heels that set off her beautiful legs so discreetly.

The man next to Jennifer Caswell sat silently fuming. He saw the P. I. looking over his girlfriend. His name was Rick Wasserman and he was the jealous type. He had a solid build, but the beginnings of a pot belly.

Kenneth Ng addressed Edward.

-Mr. Mendez? We need your help. That is why you are here.

-Forget it.

-We can no longer expose ourselves to the sunlight. Prolonged use of the brain stem serum has reduced us to the shadows and like your legendary vampires, sunlight would destroy us.

-Then, how did Antonio manage it? He was your ringleader, wasn't he?

-Yes. How quaintly you phrase that. Even he had to wear a mask not only to conceal his scarred face and true identity, but to protect himself from the sun's rays. His clothing concealed his entire body. Didn't you notice?

-And, what about his henchman: the bogey man from the fun house?

-He was not yet one of us. He could still move about freely in the daylight hours. So, you can see, Mr. Mendez, why you are here.

-Yeah. I can see all right. I did notice Miss Kawano that you stayed away from the windows until the eclipse was in full swing.

-I knew that you would notice that. But, your observation amounted to nothing.

-Where am I?

Mr. Wasserman answered.

-In a hotel on East 53rd St. It's undergoing renovations to modernize it. Don't get any ideas about escaping. You won't even if I have to kill you myself.

Edward grinned.

-That's what you think you fat bastard. I've flattened better men than you.

Miss Caswell put a restraining hand on her boyfriend.

-Rick, calm down. Mr. Mendez has every right to be angry.

Edward glared at Kenneth Ng.

-What exactly do you want from me, Mr. Ng?

-You will be – how can I phrase this? – our man on the outside.

Edward was incredulous.

-And, you'd trust me for that?

-Not completely, Mr. Mendez. We're not fools to be trifled with.

Miss Becker spoke up for the first time. Edward noticed how old this woman looked. Christ! She looked like some shriveled up prune. She was probably no raving beauty in her youth either.

-Like yourself, Mendez, we also began as outside men.

-I can believe that of you, lady. You can pass for a man.

-Bastard! How dare you!

-And, you graduated into blood suckers.

Still smarting from Edward's insult, Miss Becker addressed him.

-How crudely you put it.

Miss Becker turned to Mr. Ng.

-I don't like him, Kenneth. We shouldn't trust him. He's far too arrogant.

-He can be counted upon. His girlfriend's life depends on it. Make no mistake, we will kill her.

-I wouldn't harm her if I were you, Mr. Ng. You listening to me, pal?

-A hollow threat, Mr. Mendez.

Miss Caswell spoke up.

-Edward? We don't want to harm her. We want immortality. A few of us here are quite old. You can lead us safely to the criminal element of society. You'd be doing your law abiding citizens a service and you'd be well compensated.

-Enough of this talk. He either agrees or he doesn't. I want his answer now. We can always find someone else.

Kenneth Ng answered.

-Patience, Mr. Becker, Mr. Mendez needs a little time to think about this. It's quite a bit to take in on one's first meeting.

Mr. Ng turned his handsome face to Edward.

-But, not too long, Mr. Mendez. We're in need of stem fluid. It must be injected on a fairly regular basis or old age will begin to set in.

Edward looked about the large room. The curtains were drawn: heavy, dark curtains. What time was it? It had to be daylight outside. He wasn't unconscious for that long. He glanced at his watch: 5:30 P.M. Half the friggin' day had gone by. Christ! The sun would be close to the horizon by now and if this room were situated on the west side of the building, he'd have a chance. Would sunlight really destroy them? How? Didn't really matter so long as ti finished them off.

Mr. Ng addressed him.

-Mr. Mendez? You look lost in thought. Are you thinking over our proposal?

Edward tried stalling for time.

-I guess.

Rick Wasserman spoke.

-No time for guessing games. It's a yes or no proposition.

-Just give me a second, pal. It's a lot to digest.

-He's stalling for time.

-Mr. Mendez? Is Mr. Wasserman correct?

Edward tried not to look directly at the drawn curtains. Was that a speck of light on the rug? It was. He could see the particles of dust floating about in the air.

-May I get up and stretch, Mr. Ng?

Why did he hate calling this man by his name? This deviant didn't deserve a name. What he deserved was the god-damned "chair."

-With the help of Mr. Wasserman by your side, of course. We still do not trust you.

It had to be now. Edward got to his feet and before Mr. Wasserman could block him, he leapt across the room and pulled down the curtains.

The light from the windows flooded into the large room like a blast of lethal radiation, permeating every corner and crevice. The sun's rays touched the six cult members who were now blinded by its light. Their hands and faces caught fire and this fire spread to every part of their bodies while setting their clothes ablaze. The flames were bright orange and for a few seconds, they formed an outer skin about each cult member. Their flesh burnt away and fell in heaps to the floor. Their bodies were being turned into burning skeletal fragments. The smell of burnt flesh was nauseating.

Edward tried not to pass out. He had to find Yolanda and get out of there fast.

Kenneth Ng's face was a melted mass of disfigurement. He was blind and dying. He somehow managed to stagger to his feet as Edward pushed past him. The P. I. spotted a door in the corner of the room. He made straight for it. Jack said that Yolanda was being held in a room in this main area – this had to be the one.

And, then, the drapes that Edward had ripped off caught fire. The burning remains of Mr. Wasserman had set them ablaze.

Edward reached the door. Locked. He banged on it.

-Yolanda! Are you in there?

-Edward? Yes. They locked me in here. What's going on out there?

The fire was spreading quickly. The room was filling up with thick columns of smoke and the air was burning hot.

-Yolanda, stand back!

He kicked the door in and his girlfriend almost fell into his arms. She was frightened but unharmed. For just a second, she clung to him.

-We gotta' get out of here, baby. The place is going up like a friggin' Roman candle.

-Edward, I can barely breathe. The heat-

-Come on. We'll try for that door where they brought me in.

They made their way through the burning room, stepping over burnt flesh and bone and turned over furniture. The entire west wall was on fire and the flames were licking across the ceiling. They made it to the door just as part of the ceiling caved in. Edward tried the door knob and burned his hand turning it, but got it open.

-Edward! Your hand!

-I'm okay. I left Jack in this closet. We've gotta take him with us.

Edward flung open the closet door. Yolanda screamed. Jack Marino had hung himself in despair and guilt. An innocent boy had been used by deviants.

-Down the hall. And, that better be a fire exit up ahead.

It was. They ran down the five flights of stairs as smoke began to stream into the stairwell. They made it down the first flight when they heard a scuffing noise a few feet above them. Mr. Ng lunged at the couple. He was as good as dead and blind, but sheer grit and vengeance drove him on. Edward pushed Yolanda out of harm's way and side-stepped Mr. Ng's dive at him. He grabbed the criminal and shoved him down the next flight of stairs where Mr. Ng collapsed in a smoldering mass of flesh. Edward grabbed Yolanda and, avoiding Mr. Ng's body, they rushed down the remaining flights of stairs.

In a couple of minutes, they were at ground level and made their way out into the street. They looked up and saw flames shooting out of the hotel windows.

-They must have turned the damned sprinkler system off during renovations.

-That wasn't too smart of them.

-It might be for the best, baby. A sprinkler system in place just might have saved those bastards.

The fire engines arrived along with the police. Edward took Yolanda over to the squad car.

-We've got a story for you, officer. But, first, we need a lift to my girlfriend's place.

Lt. Donovan was looking over the wire report. The case on Missy Wingate andJohn and Erica Mills was officially closed. Josef Antonio and his henchman had been killed and Antonio's followers perished in the mid-town hotel fire. All suspects accounted for and the victims put to rest. The lab boys were still working on a couple of cadavers with a special interest directed at the brain stems. According to Dr. Ingram, a whole new branch of research was now opening up in medicine. Even she was excited about the prospect.

So, why did Lieutenant William Donovan feel unsettled? He knew why: one murder was still unresolved and the case was about to be officially closed: Dolores Sarney. Lt. Donovan knew that Edward Mendez and his girlfriend knew a whole lot more than they were letting on. And, one way or another, he'd get them as accessories. But, how? In the name of heaven…how?

Marlena Lake's daughter, Susan? Would she inform on her mother? Doubtful. No. And, then, it came to him. Of course…the good ole' police method of a "plant." And, he knew just the police woman for the job: Miss Raymond: a police officer and stand-in stenographer who Lt. Donovan had trained. He had her paged.

Chapter Ten
Sunday, September 19, 1948
Evening at Marlena's

IT WAS a Sunday evening at Marlena's Lake's town house. Marlena, Susan, Edward, and Yolanda just finished dinner and were relaxing over coffee in the living room.

-Edward, dear boy, are there any more of those deviants lurking about?

-You mean, bogeymen, don't you, mother?

Edward laughed and lit a cigarette.

-I'd say no, Marlena. I think we got 'em all. There's pretty much nothing left of them.

-Well done. And, the actual process of extracting the brain stem fluid and mixing it with...

-God only knows. Dr. Ingram thought it might be blood mixed with some chemical..

-More likely a form of plasma. I've searched Mr. Antonio's room just in case he inadvertently left anything behind.

-And?

-Nothing. He was a man who covered his tracks.

-And, Marlena, when did he move out?

-The day after Tommy Burton's murder. He arranged the seance with Miss Kawano and, then, simply left.

Susan spoke up.

-And, good riddance to him. Interesting, he was; but, I never trusted him. As a matter of fact, I was afraid of him and his disguises.

Yolanda put her coffee cup down.

-He sounds like a real creep. A man dressed up as a woman...why a woman and not just a disguise as another man?

Edward answered that one.

-No one would ever make the connection between Antonio and a Miss Himmel. This man was cunning. And, as for Miss Kawano and her cohorts...the world is a better place without them — and, that's for damned sure.

Susan laughed.

-Edward, I couldn't have put it better.

-Thanks, Susan. But, Marlena?

-Yes, dear boy?

-You mentioned something about the end of the world at that sham séance the other day.

-I did allude to it, didn't I?

-Would you mind explaining it? If the end of the world's coming, I'd like to know about it. But, I oughta' let you know that I've got a heads up from a Professor Frank Moreland.

-I know of him. He's taken over Professor Lange's position. What did he say?

Edward gave his hostess a cheshire cat smile.

-Oh...that the end of the world might not be too far away.

Yolanda spoke up and she was distressed.

-But, we just saved the world back in December. What are we facing now? It's not fair.

-That was the second time we saved this rather fragile world, my dear.

Susan put down her coffee cup.

-Mother, please don't keep us in suspense. Is there a third time coming? Please say no. Please. And, I'm with Yolanda: it's just not fair. I'm still not recovered from the last time.

Marlena lit herself a Cuban cigar; a new habit of hers.

-We're not certain of anything just yet.

-Who's "we," Marlena?

-An Iranian scientist who I've been in contact with, Edward.

Susan sat forward in her armchair.

-So, that's who you've been corresponding with these past months at the Iranian embassy. I was wondering about those letters to Iran.

Marlena continued with her explanation.

-Last December, when the sun disappeared, the earth drifted slightly out of its orbit.

Edward took a deep drag on his cigarette.

-Is that why the summer was so damned cold?

-It's a strong possibility. My contact in Iran tells me that we won't know the full extent of the earth's disrupted orbit until the end of December. The earth will have then made a full circuit in its orbit about the sun. We'll know then for certain.

Edward grinned.

-I can't wait.

Yolanda held on to Edward's free hand.

-So, Marlena, no more warm summers. Or is it worse than that? It must be.

Marlena took a puff on her cigar.

-As I've said, we don't know. It would be speculation to say otherwise.

Edward was getting a little impatient with his hostess.

-Then, guess, damn it! Don't tell me that your Iranian scientist doesn't have any theories. All scientists do. They thrive on 'em. Moreland was just full of theories that would scare the crap out of anyone.

-Our orbit may stay a bit distant from the sun or it could even correct itself.

Edward smiled at his hostess.

-Keep talking.

-Or the earth could spiral further and further away from the sun. It could even go into an extended elliptical orbit. For now, we must be patient and wait. We really don't have any choice.

-That's pretty much what Professor Moreland told me the other day. That makes two scientists agreeing on opposite sides of the ocean. I don't like that.

Edward kept looking pointedly at Marlena. He took a last drag on his cigarette before putting it out.

Susan was tempted to ask for a drag on her mother's cigar; the aroma was quite delicious. Instead, she had to make a comment.

-Any more good news, mother?

Epilogue

EILEEN KOBE was close to hysterics. Her body had gone cold with fear and a feeling of utter helplessness engulfed her.

-It's gone.

-This is impossible.

-It was in the strong box. You saw me put it there not half an hour ago. I took it out of the hat box.

-You did. The one you so carelessly carried about with you in midtown Manhattan the other day.

-That wasn't my fault.

-Wasn't it? Who else has been in this room?

-No one. I don't know...someone obviously.

-You know what this means, don't you.

-Yes.

-Tell me.

-I don't dare think about it. The gem that we stole has got to be found.

-Gem? You call it that? And, it belonged to no one.

-It's priceless.

Louis Octavio sat back in the armchair and stretched his legs.

-I don't know about that. There are those who could put quite an impressive price tag on it. I would if I had the choice.

-What are we to do? What can we do?

-Keep our wits about us and find it. The person who took it can't have gotten very far. Who could have known about it? Think, Miss Kobe. Take a few deep breaths if you must; but, think!

The woman put down the strong box and moved over to the open window. The impressive view of Central Park did not comfort nor distract her. Why had they left the room?

The man walked over to the table and slammed down the lid of the lead lined strong box. Why had they ever trusted this fool of a woman?

-That "gem" is worth millions.

Still staring out the window, the woman placed her hands to her face...almost in a gesture of prayer.

-I know. I know.

-Whoever took it must know of its value and risks. And, it may be closer than we imagine. What do you think, Miss Kobe? Should we form a search party?

The woman turned to face the man...the man who never took off his gloves. She knew why. Miss Kobe also thought she knew who might have taken the gem. If she were correct, she might be able to get it back; but it would have to be tonight. Did she dare tell this to Mr. Octavio? No. He would kill the man.

-Not close enough. But, what will they do with it? What can they do with it? And, do they know the risks? Maybe, they don't.

-You're referring to more than one person who may be our thief? "They" might destroy it. Break it down to its basic components and auction it off to any and every high bidder. What an international war game that would be: a Mexican stand off like no other. Pray they do not take it into their heads to destroy it, Miss Kobe.

-Oh,God! But, if it's not harnessed properly...

-Yes. It could obliterate the entire city of New York...or it could be released into the atmosphere and trigger off a chain reaction that would be the end of everything.

Next

The Deadliest Game

An Edward Mendez, P. I. Thriller

Book V

About the Author

GERARD DENZA has worked in the Publicity Dept. at Random House and Little, Brown, and Company in New York City. He's worked with such authors as Pete Hamill, Arthur C. Clarke, Willie Morris, and Kevin and Todd Berger.

He's the playwright and director of six Off-Off Broadway plays that include: ICARUS, MAHLER: THE MAN WHO WAS NEVER BORN, THE DYING GOD: A VAMPIRE'S TALE, SHADOWS BEHIND THE FOOTLIGHTS, and THE HOUSEDRESS. His noir play, EDMUND: THE LIKELY, has been recorded for radio broadcast. He is also the author of ICARUS: THE COLLECTED PLAYS, RAMSAY: DEALER OF DEATH, THE TIME DECEIVER: AN EDWARD MENDEZ, P. I. THRILLER, NIGHT DRIFTER, AN EDWARD MENDEZ, P. I. THRILLER, and THE IMMORTAL, AN EDWARD MENDEZ, P. I. THRILLER.

Mr. Denza is a graduate of Fordham University at Lincoln Center where he majored in psychology and graduated with honors: Magna Cum Laude.

He lives in New York City and is hard at work on his next novel: THE DEADLIEST GAME: AN EDWARD MENDEZ, P. I. THRILLER, BOOK V.